Tales of Mystery and Terror

EDGAR ALLAN POE (1809–49) was born in Boston. Both his parents were actors of no great renown; both suffered from tuberculosis; and both died in 1811. Young Edgar Poe was taken in by John Allan, a wealthy merchant – hence his middle name.

He had a happy childhood as the only child of a prosperous family, and he excelled at school in languages and athletics. Then in 1826 he went to the University of Virginia. He spent his first term on wine, women and song – and provoked a massive row with his step-father, which ended with Poe running away and joining the army (under the name of Edgar A. Perry).

A few years later, Mrs Allan begged her husband, on her death-bed, to find their estranged son. He did, but after her death the relationship between the two men did not improve. Allan remarried and his new wife hated Edgar.

By 1831 Poe was out in the world, alone, the destitute author of three volumes of poetry which hardly anyone was reading. Then he found a kind of family. He discovered an aunt, Maria Clemm, and he made her a surrogate mother; he also married her daughter, his cousin Virginia, in 1837, when she was only fourteen years old.

The family moved around from place to place, as Edgar found and lost jobs. Occasionally he got a story printed, but the pay was terrible, and they were often freezing and close to starving. Virginia was by now critically ill – and Poe was virtually an alcoholic.

In 1847, Virginia died, and Edgar Poe began a round of courting wealthy widows: he was sometimes engaged to several at once. His writing – especially his poetry – grew more tortured. 'I dwelt alone in a world of moan,' he said. In short, he was more or less mad, and he was still drinking.

George Bernard Shaw rated him 'the finest of finest of artists'; but he died alone, in pain and squalor. Almost his last words were: 'I wish to God someone would blow my damned brains out.' It is not difficult to see why some of his best stories are the grotesque and macabre tales in this volume.

Some other Puffin Classics to enjoy

LORNA DOONE
R. D. Blackmore

JANE EYRE
Charlotte Brontë

WUTHERING HEIGHTS
Emily Brontë

A CHRISTMAS CAROL
GREAT EXPECTATIONS
Charles Dickens

EDGAR ALLAN POE

Tales of Mystery and Terror

PUFFIN BOOKS

PUFFIN BOOKS

Published by the Penguin Group
Penguin Books Ltd, 27 Wrights Lane, London W8 5TZ, England
Penguin Books USA Inc., 375 Hudson Street, New York, New York 10014, USA
Penguin Books Australia Ltd, Ringwood, Victoria, Australia
Penguin Books Canada Ltd, 10 Alcorn Avenue, Toronto, Ontario, Canada M4V 3B2
Penguin Books (NZ) Ltd, 182–190 Wairau Road, Auckland 10, New Zealand

Penguin Books Ltd, Registered Offices: Harmondsworth, Middlesex, England

This collection published in Puffin Books 1990
Reissued in this edition 1994
12

Filmset by Datix International Limited, Bungay, Suffolk
Printed in England by Clays Ltd, St Ives plc
Set in 12/15 pt Monophoto Plantin

Contents

THE SPHINX

During the dread reign of cholera in New York, I had accepted the invitation of a relative to spend a fortnight with him in the retirement of his *cottage ornée* on the banks of the Hudson. We had here around us all the ordinary means of summer amusement; and what with rambling in the woods, sketching, boating, fishing, bathing, music, and books, we should have passed the time pleasantly enough, but for the fearful intelligence which reached us every morning from the populous city. Not a day elapsed which did not bring us news of the decease of some acquaintance. Then, as the fatality increased, we learned to expect daily the loss of some friend. At length we trembled at the approach of every messenger. The very air from the South seemed to us redolent with death. That palsying thought, indeed, took entire possession of my soul. I could neither speak, think, nor dream of anything else. My host was of a less excitable temperament, and, although greatly depressed in spirits, exerted himself to sustain my own. His richly philosophical intellect was not at any time affected by unrealities. To the substances of terror he was sufficiently alive, but of its shadows he had no apprehension.

His endeavors to arouse me from the condition of abnormal gloom into which I had fallen, were frustrated, in great measure, by certain volumes which I had found in his library. These were of a character to force into germination whatever seeds of hereditary superstition lay latent in my bosom. I had been reading these books without his knowledge, and thus he was often at a loss to account for the forcible impressions which had been made upon my fancy.

A favorite topic with me was the popular belief in omens – a belief which, at this one epoch of my life, I was almost seriously disposed to defend. On this subject we had long and animated discussions; he maintaining the utter groundlessness of faith in such matters, I contending that a popular sentiment arising with absolute spontaneity – that is to say, without apparent traces of suggestion – had in itself the unmistakable elements of truth, and was entitled to much respect.

The fact is, that soon after my arrival at the cottage there had occurred to myself an incident so entirely inexplicable, and which had in it so much of the portentous character, that I might well have been excused for regarding it as an omen. It appalled, and at the same time so confounded and bewildered me, that many days elapsed before I could make up my mind to communicate the circumstance to my friend.

Near the close of an exceedingly warm day, I was sitting, book in hand, at an open window, commanding, through a long vista of the river banks, a view of a distant hill, the face of which nearest my position had been denuded by what is termed a landslide, of the principal portion of its trees. My thoughts had been long wandering from the volume before me to the gloom and desolation of the neighboring city. Uplifting my eyes from the page, they fell upon the naked face of the hill, and upon an object – upon some living monster of hideous conformation, which very rapidly made its way from the summit to the bottom, disappearing finally in the dense forest below. As this creature first came in sight, I doubted my own sanity – or at least the evidence of my own eyes – and many minutes passed before I succeeded in convincing myself that I was neither mad nor in a dream. Yet when I describe the monster (which I distinctly saw, and calmly surveyed through the whole period of its progress), my readers, I fear, will feel more difficulty in being convinced of these points than even I did myself.

Estimating the size of the creature by comparison with the diameter of the large trees near which it passed – the few giants of the forests which had escaped the fury of the landslide – I concluded it to be far larger than any ship of the line in existence. I say ship of the line, because the shape of the monster suggested the idea – the hull of one of our seventy-fours might convey a very tolerable conception of the general outline. The mouth of the animal was situated at the extremity of a proboscis some sixty or seventy feet in length, and about as thick as the body of an ordinary elephant. Near the root of this trunk was an immense quantity of black shaggy hair – more than could have been supplied by the coats of a score of buffaloes; and projecting from this hair downwardly and laterally, sprang two gleaming tusks not unlike those of the wild boar, but of infinitely greater dimension. Extending forward, parallel with the proboscis, and on each side of it, was a gigantic staff, thirty or forty feet in length, formed seemingly of pure crystal, and in shape a perfect prism – it reflected in the most gorgeous manner the rays of the declining sun. The trunk was fashioned like a wedge with the apex to the earth. From it there were outspread two pairs of wings – each wing nearly one hundred yards in length – one pair being placed above the other, and all thickly covered with metal scales; each scale apparently some ten or twelve feet in diameter. I observed that the upper and lower tiers of wings were connected by a strong chain. But the chief peculiarity of this horrible thing was the representation of a *Death's Head*, which covered nearly the whole surface of its breast, and which was as accurately traced in glaring white, upon the dark ground of the body, as if it had been there carefully designed by an artist. When I regarded this terrific animal, and more especially the appearance on its breast, with a feeling of horror and awe – with a sentiment of forthcoming evil, which I found it impossible to quell by any effort of the reason, I perceived the huge jaws at the extremity of the proboscis suddenly expand themselves, and from them there proceeded a sound so loud and so expressive of woe, that it struck upon my nerves like a knell, and as the monster disappeared at the foot of the hill, I fell at once, fainting, to the floor.

Upon recovering, my first impulse, of course, was to inform my friend of what I had seen and heard – and I can scarcely explain what feeling of repugnance it was which, in the end, operated to prevent me.

At length, one evening, some three or four days after the occurrence, we were sitting together in the room in which I had seen the apparition – I occupying the same seat at the same window, and he lounging on a sofa near at hand. The association of the place and time impelled me to give him an account of the phenomenon. He heard me to the end – at first laughed heartily – and then lapsed into an excessively grave demeanor, as if my insanity was a thing beyond suspicion. At this instant I again had a distinct view of the monster – to which, with a shout of absolute terror, I now directed his attention. He looked eagerly – but maintained that he saw nothing – although I designated minutely the course of the creature, as it made its way down the naked face of the hill.

I was now immeasurably alarmed, for I considered the vision either as an omen of my death, or, worse, as the forerunner of an attack of mania. I threw myself passionately back in my chair, and for some moments buried my face in my hands. When I uncovered my eyes, the apparition was no longer visible.

My host, however, had in some degree resumed the calmness of his demeanor, and questioned me very rigorously in respect to the conformation of the visionary creature. When I had fully satisfied him on this head, he sighed deeply, as if relieved of some intolerable burden, and went on to talk, with what I thought a cruel calmness, of various points of speculative philosophy, which had heretofore formed subject of discussion between us. I remember his insisting very especially (among other things) upon the idea that the principal source of error in all human investigations lay in the liability of the understanding to underrate or to overvalue the importance of an object, through mere misadmeasurement of its propinquity. 'To estimate properly, for example,' he said, 'the influence to be exercised on mankind at large by the thorough diffusion of Democracy, the distance of the epoch at which such diffusion may possibly be accomplished should not fail to form an item in the estimate. Yet can you tell me one writer on the subject of government who has ever thought this particular branch of the subject worthy of discussion at all?'

He here paused for a moment, stepped to a bookcase, and brought forth one of the ordinary synopses of Natural History. Requesting me then to exchange seats with him, that he might the better distinguish the fine print of the volume, he took my armchair at the window, and, opening the book, resumed his discourse very much in the same tone as before.

'But for your exceeding minuteness,' he said, 'in describing the monster, I might never have had it in my power to demonstrate to you what it was. In the first place, let me read to you a schoolboy account of the genus *Sphinx*, of the family of *Crepuscularia*, of the order *Lepidoptera*, of the class of *Insecta* – or insects. The account runs thus:

'"Four membranous wings covered with little colored scales of metallic appearance; mouth forming a rolled proboscis, produced by an elongation of the jaws, upon the sides of which are found the rudiments of mandibles and downy palpi; the inferior wings retained to the superior by a stiff hair, antennae in the form of an elongated club, prismatic; abdomen pointed. The Death's-headed Sphinx has occasioned much terror among the vulgar, at times, by the melancholy kind of cry which it utters, and the insignia of death which it wears upon its corslet."'

He here closed the book and leaned forward in the chair, placing himself accurately in the position which I had occupied at the moment of beholding 'the monster'.

'Ah, here it is,' he presently exclaimed – 'it is reascending the face of the hill, and a very remarkable looking creature I admit it to be. Still, it is by no means so large or so distant as you imagined it; for the fact is that, as it wriggles its way up this thread, which some spider has wrought along the window-sash, I find it to be about the sixteenth of an inch in its extreme length, and also about the sixteenth of an inch distant from the pupil of my eye.'

The Fall of the House of Usher

Son coeur est un luth suspendu;
Sitôt qu'on le touche il résonne.

– De Béranger

During the whole of a dull, dark, and soundless day in the autumn of the year, when the clouds hung oppressively low in the heavens, I had been passing alone, on horseback, through a singularly dreary tract of country, and at length found myself, as the shades of the evening drew on, within view of the melancholy House of Usher. I know not how it was – but, with the first glimpse of the building, a sense of insufferable gloom pervaded my spirit. I say insufferable; for the feeling was unrelieved by any of that half-pleasurable, because poetic, sentiment with which the mind usually receives even the sternest natural images of the desolate or terrible. I looked upon the scene before me – upon the mere house, and the simple landscape features of the domain – upon the bleak walls – upon the vacant eye-like windows – upon a few rank sedges – and upon a few white trunks of decayed trees – with an utter depression of soul which I can compare to no earthly sensation more properly than to the after-dream of the reveller upon opium – the bitter lapse into everyday life – the hideous dropping off of the veil. There was an iciness, a sinking, a sickening of the heart – an unredeemed dreariness of thought which no goading of the imagination could torture into aught of the sublime. What was it – I paused to think – what was it that so unnerved me in the contemplation of the House of Usher? It was a mystery all insoluble; nor could I grapple with the shadowy fancies that crowded upon me as I pondered. I was forced to fall back upon the unsatisfactory conclusion, that while, beyond doubt, there *are* combinations of very simple natural objects which have the power of thus affecting us, still the analysis of this power lies among considerations beyond our depth. It was possible, I reflected, that a mere different arrangement of the particulars of the scene, of the details of the picture, would be sufficient to modify, or perhaps to annihilate its capacity for sorrowful impression; and, acting upon this idea, I reined my horse to the precipitous brink of a black and lurid tarn that lay in unruffled lustre by the dwelling, and gazed down – but with a shudder even more thrilling than before – upon the remod-elled and inverted images of the gray sedge, and the ghastly tree-stems, and the vacant and eye-like windows.

Nevertheless, in this mansion of gloom I now proposed to myself a sojourn of some weeks. Its proprietor, Roderick Usher, had been one of my boon companions in boyhood; but many years had elapsed since our last meeting. A letter, however, had lately reached me in a distant part of the country – a letter from him – which, in its wildly importunate nature, had admitted of no other than a personal reply. The MS gave evidence of nervous agitation. The writer spoke of acute bodily illness – of a mental disorder which oppressed him – and of an earnest desire to see me, as his best and indeed his only personal friend, with a view of attempting, by the cheerfulness of my society, some alleviation of his malady. It was the manner in which all this, and much more, was said – it was the apparent *heart* that went with his request – which allowed me no room for hesitation; and I accordingly obeyed forthwith what I still considered a very singular summons.

Although, as boys, we had been even intimate associates, yet I really knew little of my friend. His reserve had been always excessive and habitual. I was aware, however, that his very ancient family had been noted, time out of mind, for a peculiar sensibility of temperament, displaying itself, through long ages, in many works of exalted art, and manifested, of late, in repeated deeds of munificent yet unobtrusive charity, as well as in a passionate devotion to the intricacies, perhaps even more than to the orthodox and easily recognizable beauties, of musical science. I had learned, too, the very remarkable fact, that the stem of the Usher race, all time-honored as it was, had put forth, at no period, any enduring branch; in other words, that the entire family lay in the direct line of descent, and had always, with very trifling and very temporary variation, so lain. It was this deficiency, I considered, while running over in thought the perfect keeping of the character of the premises with the accredited character of the people, and while speculating upon the possible influence which the one, in the long lapse of centuries, might have exercised upon the other – it was this deficiency, perhaps, of collateral issue, and the consequent undeviating transmission, from sire to son, of the patrimony with the name, which had, at length, so identified the two as to merge the original title of the estate in the quaint and equivocal appellation of the 'House of Usher' – an appellation which seemed to include, in the minds of the peasantry who used it, both the family and the family mansion.

I have said that the sole effect of my somewhat childish experiment – that of looking down within the tarn – had been to deepen the first singular impression. There can be no doubt that the consciousness of the rapid increase of my superstition – for why should I not so term it? – served mainly to accelerate the increase itself. Such, I have long known, is the paradoxical law of all sentiments having terror as a basis. And it might have been for this reason only, that, when I again uplifted my eyes to the house itself, from its image in the pool, there grew in my mind a strange fancy – a fancy so ridiculous, indeed, that I but mention it to show the vivid force of the sensations which oppressed me. I had so worked upon my imagination as really to believe that about the whole mansion and domain there hung an atmosphere peculiar to themselves and their immediate vicinity – an atmosphere which had no affinity with the air of heaven, but which had reeked up from the decayed trees, and the gray wall, and the silent tarn – a pestilent and mystic vapor, dull, sluggish, faintly discernible, and leaden-hued.

Shaking off from my spirit what *must* have been a dream, I scanned more narrowly the real aspect of the building. Its principal feature seemed to be that of an excessive antiquity. The discoloration of ages had been great. Minute fungi overspread the whole exterior, hanging in a fine tangled web-work from the eaves. Yet all this was apart from any extraordinary dilapidation. No portion of the masonry had fallen; and there appeared to be a wild inconsistency between its still perfect adaptation of parts, and the crumbling condition of the individual stones. In this there was much that reminded me of the specious totality of old wood-work which has rotted for long years in some neglected vault, with no disturbance from the breath of the external air. Beyond this indication of extensive decay, however, the fabric gave little token of instability. Perhaps the eye of a scrutinizing observer might have discovered a barely perceptible fissure, which, extending from the roof of the building in front, made its way down the wall in a zigzag direction, until it became lost in the sullen waters of the tarn.

Noticing these things, I rode over a short causeway to the house. A servant in waiting took my horse, and I entered the Gothic archway of the hall. A valet, of stealthy step, thence conducted me, in silence, through many dark and intricate passages in my progress to the *studio* of his master. Much that I encountered on the way contributed, I know not how, to heighten the vague sentiments of which I have already spoken. While the objects around me – while the carvings of the ceilings, the sombre tapestries of the walls, the ebon blackness of the floors, and the phantasmagoric armorial trophies which rattled as I strode, were but matters to which, or to such as which, I had been accustomed from my infancy – while I hesitated not to acknowledge how familiar was all this – I still wondered to find how unfamiliar were the fancies which ordinary images were stirring up. On one of the staircases, I met the physician of the family. His countenance, I thought, wore a mingled expression of low cunning and perplexity. He accosted me with trepidation and passed on. The valet now threw open a door and ushered me into the presence of his master.

The room in which I found myself was very

large and lofty. The windows were long, narrow, and pointed, and at so vast a distance from the black oaken floor as to be altogether inaccessible from within. Feeble gleams of encrimsoned light made their way through the trellised panes, and served to render sufficiently distinct the more prominent objects around; the eye, however, struggled in vain to reach the remoter angles of the chamber, or the recesses of the vaulted and fretted ceiling. Dark draperies hung upon the walls. The general furniture was profuse, comfortless, antique, and tattered. Many books and musical instruments lay scattered about, but failed to give any vitality to the scene. I felt that I breathed an atmosphere of sorrow. An air of stern, deep, and irredeemable gloom hung over and pervaded all.

Upon my entrance, Usher arose from a sofa on which he had been lying at full length, and greeted me with a vivacious warmth which had much in it, I at first thought, of an overdone cordiality – of the constrained effort of the *ennuyé* man of the world. A glance, however, at his countenance convinced me of his perfect sincerity. We sat down; and for some moments, while he spoke not, I gazed upon him with a feeling half of pity, half of awe. Surely, man had never before so terribly altered, in so brief a period, as had Roderick Usher! It was with difficulty that I could bring myself to admit the identity of the wan being before me with the companion of my early boyhood. Yet the character of his face had been at all times remarkable. A cadaverousness of complexion; an eye large, liquid, and luminous beyond comparison; lips somewhat thin and very pallid but of a surpassingly beautiful curve; a nose of a delicate Hebrew model, but with a breadth of nostril unusual in similar formations; a finely moulded chin, speaking, in its want of prominence, of a want of moral energy; hair of a more than web-like softness and tenuity; these features, with an inordinate expansion above the regions of the temple, made up altogether a countenance not easily to be forgotten. And now in the mere exaggeration of the prevailing character of these features, and of the expression they were wont to convey, lay so much of change that I doubted to whom I spoke. The now ghastly pallor of the skin, and the now miraculous lustre of the eye, above all things startled and even awed me. The silken hair, too, had been suffered to grow all unheeded, and as, in its wild gossamer texture, it floated rather than fell about the face, I could not, even with effort, connect its Arabesque expression with any idea of simple humanity.

In the manner of my friend I was at once struck with an incoherence – an inconsistency; and I soon found this to arise from a series of feeble and futile struggles to overcome an habitual trepidancy – an excessive nervous agitation. For something of this nature I had indeed been prepared, no less by his letter, than by reminiscences of certain boyish traits, and by conclusions deduced from his peculiar physical conformation and temperament. His action was alternately vivacious and sullen. His voice varied rapidly from a tremulous indecision (when the animal spirits seemed utterly in abeyance) to that species of energetic concision – that abrupt, weighty, unhurried, and hollow-sounding enunciation – that leaden, self-balanced, and perfectly modulated guttural utterance, which may be observed in the lost drunkard, or the irreclaimable eater of opium, during the periods of his most intense excitement.

It was thus that he spoke of the object of my visit, of his earnest desire to see me, and of the solace he expected me to afford him. He entered, at some length, into what he conceived to be the nature of his malady. It was, he said, a constitutional and a family evil, and one for which he despaired to find a remedy – a mere nervous affection, he immediately added, which would undoubtedly soon pass off. It displayed itself in a host of unnatural sensations. Some of these, as he detailed them, interested and bewildered me; although, perhaps, the terms and the general manner of their narration had their weight. He suffered much from a morbid acuteness of the senses; the most insipid food was alone endurable; he could wear only garments of certain texture; the odors of all flowers were oppressive; his eyes were tortured by even a faint light; and there were but peculiar sounds, and these from stringed instruments, which did not inspire him with horror.

To an anomalous species of terror I found him a bounden slave. 'I shall perish,' said he, 'I *must* perish in this deplorable folly. Thus, thus, and not otherwise, shall I be lost. I dread the events of the future, not in themselves, but in their results. I shudder at the thought of any, even the most trivial, incident, which may operate upon this intolerable agitation of soul. I have, indeed, no abhorrence of danger, except in its absolute effect – in terror. In this unnerved, in this pitiable, condition I feel that the period will sooner or later arrive when I must abandon life and reason together, in some struggle with the grim phantasm, FEAR.'

I learned, moreover, at intervals, and through broken and equivocal hints, another singular feature of his mental condition. He was enchained by certain superstitious impressions in regard to the dwelling which he tenanted, and whence, for many years, he had never ventured forth – in regard to an influence whose supposititious force was conveyed in terms too shadowy here to be re-stated – an influence which some peculiarities in the mere form and substance of his family mansion had, by dint of long sufferance, he said, obtained over his spirit – an effect which the *physique* of the gray walls and turrets, and of the dim tarn into which they all looked down, had, at length, brought about upon the *morale* of his existence.

He admitted, however, although with hesitation, that much of the peculiar gloom which thus afflicted him could be traced to a more natural and far more palpable origin – to the severe and long-continued illness – indeed to the evidently approaching dissolution – of a tenderly beloved sister, his sole companion for long years, his last and only relative on earth. 'Her decease,' he said, with a bitterness which I can never forget, 'would leave him (him the hopeless and the frail) the last of the ancient race of the Ushers.' While he spoke, the lady Madeline (for so was she called) passed through a remote portion of the apartment, and, without having noticed my presence, disappeared. I regarded her with an utter astonishment not unmingled with dread; and yet I found it impossible to account for such feelings. A sensation of stupor oppressed me as my eyes followed her retreating steps. When a door, at length, closed upon her, my glance sought instinctively and eagerly the countenance of the brother; but he had buried his face in his hands, and I could only perceive that a far more than ordinary wanness had overspread the emaciated fingers through which trickled many passionate tears.

The disease of the lady Madeline had long baffled the skill of her physicians. A settled apathy, a gradual wasting away of the person, and frequent although transient affections of a partially cataleptical character were the unusual diagnosis. Hitherto she had steadily borne up against the pressure of her malady; and had not betaken herself finally to bed; but on the closing in of the evening of my arrival at the house, she succumbed (as her brother told me at night with inexpressible agitation) to the prostrating power of the destroyer; and I learned that the glimpse I had obtained of her person would thus probably be the last I should obtain – that the lady, at least while living, would be seen by me no more.

For several days ensuing, her name was unmentioned by either Usher or myself; and during this period I was busied in earnest endeavors to alleviate the melancholy of my friend. We painted and read together, or I listened, as if in a dream, to the wild improvisations of his speaking guitar. And thus, as a closer and still closer intimacy admitted me more unreservedly into the recesses of his spirit, the more bitterly did I perceive the futility of all attempt at cheering a mind from which darkness, as if an inherent positive quality, poured forth upon all objects of the moral and physical universe in one unceasing radiation of gloom.

I shall ever bear about me a memory of the many solemn hours I thus spent alone with the master of the House of Usher. Yet I should fail in any attempt to convey an idea of the exact character of the studies, or of the occupations, in which he involved me, or led me the way. An excited and highly distempered ideality threw a sulphureous lustre over all. His long improvised dirges will ring for ever in my ears. Among other things, I hold painfully in mind a certain singular perver-

sion and amplification of the wild air of the last
waltz of Von Weber. From the paintings over
which his elaborate fancy brooded, and which
grew, touch by touch, into vaguenesses at which I
shuddered the more thrillingly, because I shuddered knowing not why – from these paintings
(vivid as their images now are before me) I would
in vain endeavor to educe more than a small
portion which should lie within the compass of
merely written words. By the utter simplicity, by
the nakedness of his designs, he arrested and over-
awed attention. If ever mortal painted an idea,
that mortal was Roderick Usher. For me at least,
in the circumstances then surrounding me, there
arose out of the pure abstractions which the hypochondriac contrived to throw upon his canvas, an
intensity of intolerable awe, no shadow of which
felt I ever yet in the contemplation of the certainly
glowing yet too concrete reveries of Fuseli.

One of the phantasmagoric conceptions of my
friend, partaking not so rigidly of the spirit of
abstraction, may be shadowed forth, although
feebly, in words. A small picture presented the
interior of an immensely long and rectangular vault
or tunnel, with low walls, smooth, white, and
without interruption or device. Certain accessory
points of the design served well to convey the idea
that this excavation lay at an exceeding depth below
the surface of the earth. No outlet was observed in
any portion of its vast extent, and no torch or other
artificial source of light was discernible; yet a flood

of intense rays rolled throughout, and bathed the whole in a ghastly and inappropriate splendor.

I have just spoken of that morbid condition of the auditory nerve which rendered all music intolerable to the sufferer, with the exception of certain effects of stringed instruments. It was, perhaps, the narrow limits to which he thus confined himself upon the guitar which gave birth, in great measure, to the fantastic character of his performances. But the fervid *facility* of his *impromptus* could not be so accounted for. They must have been, and were, in the notes, as well as in the words of his wild fantasias (for he not unfrequently accompanied himself with rhymed verbal improvisations), the result of that intense mental collectedness and concentration to which I have previously alluded as observable only in particular moments of the highest artificial excitement. The words of one of these rhapsodies I have easily remembered. I was, perhaps, the more forcibly impressed with it as he gave it, because, in the under or mystic current of its meaning, I fancied that I perceived, and for the first time, a full consciousness on the part of Usher of the tottering of his lofty reason upon her throne. The verses, which were entitled 'The Haunted Palace' ran very nearly, if not accurately, thus:

I

In the greenest of our valleys,
By good angels tenanted,

Once a fair and stately palace –
    Radiant palace – reared its head.
In the monarch Thought's dominion –
    It stood there!
Never seraph spread a pinion
    Over fabric half so fair.

II

Banners yellow, glorious, golden,
    On its roof did float and flow
(This – all this – was in the olden
    Time long ago);
And every gentle air that dallied,
    In that sweet day.
Along the ramparts plumed and pallid,
    A winged odor went away.

III

Wanderers in that happy valley
    Through two luminous windows saw
Spirits moving musically
    To a lute's well-tunèd law;
Round about a throne, where sitting
    (Porphyrogene!)
In state his glory well befitting,
    The ruler of the realm was seen.

IV

And all with pearl and ruby glowing
    Was the fair palace door,
Through which came flowing, flowing, flowing

And sparkling evermore,
A troop of Echoes whose sweet duty
    Was but to sing,
In voices of surpassing beauty,
    The wit and wisdom of their king.

V

But evil things, in robes of sorrow,
    Assailed the monarch's high estate;
(Ah, let us mourn, for never morrow
    Shall dawn upon him, desolate!)
And, round about his home, the glory
    That blushed and bloomed
Is but a dim-remembered story
    Of the old time entombed.

VI

And travellers now within that valley,
    Through the red-litten windows see
Vast forms that move fantastically
    To a discordant melody;
While, like a rapid ghastly river,
    Through the pale door,
A hideous throng rush out for ever,
    And laugh – but smile no more.

I well remember that suggestions arising from
this ballad led us into a train of thought wherein
there became manifest an opinion of Usher's
which I mention not so much on account of its

novelty (for other men* have thought thus), as on account of the pertinacity with which he maintained it. This opinion, in its general form, was on account of the pertinacity with which he maintained it. This opinion, in its general form, was that of the sentience of all vegetable things. But, in his disordered fancy, the idea had assumed a more daring character, and trespassed, under certain conditions, upon the kingdom of inorganization. I lack words to express the full extent, or the earnest *abandon* of his persuasion. The belief, however, was connected (as I have previously hinted) with the gray stones of the home of his forefathers. The conditions of the sentience had been here, he imagined, fulfilled in the method of collocation of these stones – in the order of their arrangement, as well as in that of the many *fungi* which overspread them, and of the decayed trees which stood around – above all, in the long undisturbed endurance of this arrangement, and in its reduplication in the still waters of the tarn. Its evidence – the evidence of the sentience – was to be seen, he said (and I here started as he spoke), in the gradual yet certain condensation of an atmosphere of their own about the waters and the walls. The result was discoverable, he added, in that silent yet importunate and terrible influence which for centuries had moulded the destinies of

* Watson, Dr Percival, Spallanzani, and especially the Bishop of Landaff. See 'Chemical Essays', vol. v.

his family, and which made *him* what I now saw him – what he was. Such opinions need no comment, and I will make none.

Our books – the books which, for years had formed no small portion of the mental existence of the invalid – were, as might be supposed, in strict keeping with this character of phantasm. We pored together over such works as the *Ververt et Chartreuse* of Gresset; the *Belphegor* of Machiavelli; the *Heaven and Hell* of Swedenborg; the *Subterranean Voyage of Nicholas Klimm* of Holberg; the *Chiromancy* of Robert Flud, of Jean D'Indaginé, and of De la Chambre; the *Journey into the Blue Distance* of Tieck; and the *City of the Sun* of Campanella. One favorite volume was a small octavo edition of the *Directorium Inquisitorium*, by the Dominican Eymeric de Gironne; and there were passages in Pomponius Mela, about the old African Satyrs and Aegipans, over which Usher would sit dreaming for hours. His chief delight, however, was found in the perusal of an exceedingly rare and curious book in quarto Gothic – the manual of a forgotten church – the *Vigiliae Mortuorum secundum Chorum Ecclesiae Maguntinae*.

I could not help thinking of the wild ritual of this work, and of its probable influence upon the hypochondriac, when, one evening, having informed me abruptly that the lady Madeline was no more, he stated his intention of preserving her corpse for a fortnight (previously to its final interment), in one of the numerous vaults within the main walls of the building. The worldly reason, however, assigned for this singular proceeding, was one which I did not feel at liberty to dispute. The brother had been led to his resolution (so he told me) by consideration of the unusual character of the malady of the deceased, of certain obtrusive and eager inquiries on the part of her medical men, and of the remote and exposed situation of the burial-ground of the family. I will not deny that when I called to mind the sinister countenance of the person whom I met upon the staircase, on the day of my arrival at the house, I had no desire to oppose what I regarded as at best but a harmless, and by no means an unnatural, precaution.

At the request of Usher, I personally aided him in the arrangements for the temporary entomb-ment. The body having been encoffined, we two alone bore it to its rest. The vault in which we placed it (and which had been so long unopened that our torches, half smothered in its oppressive atmosphere, gave us little opportunity for investi-gation) was small, damp, and entirely without means of admission for light; lying, at great depth, immediately beneath that portion of the building in which was my own sleeping apartment. It had been used, apparently, in remote feudal times, for the worst purposes of a donjon-keep, and, in later days, as a place of deposit for powder, or some other highly combustible substance, as a portion of its floor, and the whole interior of a long archway through which we reached it, were carefully sheathed with copper. The door, of massive iron, had been, also, similarly protected. Its immense weight caused an unusually sharp, grating sound, as it moved upon its hinges.

Having deposited our mournful burden upon tressels within this region of horror, we partially turned aside the yet unscrewed lid of the coffin, and looked upon the face of the tenant. A striking similitude between the brother and sister now first arrested my attention; and Usher, divining, perhaps, my thoughts, murmured out some few words from which I learned that the deceased and himself had been twins, and that sympathies of a scarcely intelligible nature had always existed between them. Our glances, however, rested not long upon the dead – for we could not regard her unawed. The disease which had thus entombed the lady in the maturity of youth, had left, as usual in all maladies of a strictly cataleptical character, the mockery of a faint blush upon the bosom and the face, and that suspiciously lingering smile upon the lip which is so terrible in death. We replaced and screwed down the lid, and, having secured the door of iron, made our way, with toil, into the scarcely less gloomy apartments of the upper portion of the house.

And now, some days of bitter grief having elapsed, an observable change came over the features of the mental disorder of my friend. His ordinary manner had vanished. His ordinary occupations were neglected or forgotten. He roamed from chamber to chamber with hurried, unequal, and objectless step. The pallor of his countenance had assumed, if possible, a more ghastly hue – but the luminousness of his eye had utterly gone out. The once occasional huskiness of his tone was heard no more; and a tremulous quaver, as if of extreme terror, habitually characterized his utterance. There were times, indeed, when I thought his unceasingly agitated mind was laboring with some oppressive secret, to divulge which he struggled for the necessary courage. At times, again, I was obliged to resolve all into the mere inexplicable vagaries of madness, for I beheld him gazing upon vacancy for long hours, in an attitude of the profoundest attention, as if listening to some imaginary sound. It was no wonder that his condition terrified – that it infected me. I felt creeping upon me, by slow yet certain degrees, the wild influences of his own fantastic yet impressive superstitions.

It was, especially, upon retiring to bed late in the night of the seventh or eighth day after the placing of the lady Madeline within the donjon, that I experienced the full power of such feelings. Sleep came not near my couch – while the hours waned and waned away. I struggled to reason off the nervousness which had dominion over me. I endeavored to believe that much, if not all of what I felt, was due to the bewildering influence of the gloomy furniture of the room – of the dark and tattered draperies, which, tortured into motion by the breath of a rising tempest, swayed fitfully to and fro upon the walls, and rustled uneasily about the decorations of the bed. But my efforts were fruitless. An irrepressible tremor gradually pervaded my frame; and, at length, there sat upon my very heart an incubus of utterly causeless alarm. Shaking this off with a gasp and a struggle, I uplifted myself upon the pillows, and, peering earnestly within the intense darkness of the chamber, hearkened – I know not why, except that an instinctive spirit prompted me – to certain low and indefinite sounds which came, through the pauses of the storm, at long intervals, I knew not whence. Overpowered by an intense sentiment of horror, unaccountable yet unendurable, I threw on my clothes with haste (for I felt that I should sleep no more during the night), and endeavored to arouse myself from the pitiable condition into which I had fallen, by pacing rapidly to and fro through the apartment.

I had taken but few turns in this manner, when a light step on an adjoining staircase arrested my attention. I presently recognized it as that of Usher. In an instant afterward he rapped, with a gentle touch, at my door, and entered, bearing a lamp. His countenance was, as usual, cadaverously wan – but, moreover, there was a species of mad hilarity in his eyes – an evidently restrained *hysteria* in his whole demeanor. His air appalled me – but anything was preferable to the solitude which I had so long endured, and I even welcomed his presence as a relief.

'And you have not seen it?' he said abruptly,

after having stared about him for some moments in silence – 'you have not then seen it? – but, stay! you shall.' Thus speaking, and having carefully shaded his lamp, he hurried to one of the casements, and threw it freely open to the storm.

The impetuous fury of the entering gust nearly lifted us from our feet. It was, indeed, a tempestuous yet sternly beautiful night, and one wildly singular in its terror and its beauty. A whirlwind had apparently collected its force in our vicinity; for there were frequent and violent alterations in the direction of the wind; and the exceeding density of the clouds (which hung so low as to press upon the turrets of the house) did not prevent our perceiving the life-like velocity with which they flew careering from all points against each other, without passing away into the distance. I say that even their exceeding density did not prevent our perceiving this – yet we had no glimpse of the moon or stars, nor was there any flashing forth of the lightning. But the under surfaces of the huge masses of agitated vapor, as well as all terrestrial objects immediately around us, were glowing in the unnatural light of a faintly luminous and distinctly visible gaseous exhalation which hung about and enshrouded the mansion.

'You must not – you shall not behold this!' said I – shuddering, to Usher, as I led him, with a gentle violence, from the window to a seat. 'These appearances, which bewilder you, are merely electrical phenomena not uncommon – or it may be that they have their ghastly origin in the rank miasma of the tarn. Let us close this casement; the air is chilling and dangerous to your frame. Here is one of your favorite romances. I will read, and you shall listen: and so we will pass away this terrible night together.'

The antique volume which I had taken up was the *Mad Trist* of Sir Launcelot Canning; but I had called it a favorite of Usher's more in sad jest than in earnest; for, in truth, there is little in its uncouth and unimaginative prolixity which could have had interest for the lofty and spiritual ideality of my friend. It was, however, the only book immediately at hand; and I indulged a vague hope that the excitement which now agitated the hypochondriac, might find relief (for the history of mental disorder is full of similar anomalies) even in the extremeness of the folly which I should read. Could I have judged, indeed, by the wild overstrained air of vivacity with which he hearkened, or apparently hearkened, to the words of the tale, I might well have congratulated myself upon the success of my design.

I had arrived at that well-known portion of the story where Ethelred, the hero of the Trist, having sought in vain for peaceable admission into the dwelling of the hermit, proceeds to make good an entrance by force. Here, it will be remembered, the words of the narrative run thus:

'And Ethelred, who was by nature of a doughty heart, and who was now mighty withal, on account of the powerfulness of the wine which he had drunken, waited no longer to hold parley with the hermit, who, in sooth, was of an obstinate and maliceful turn, but, feeling the rain upon his shoulders, and fearing the rising of the tempest, uplifted his mace outright, and, with blows, made quickly room in the plankings of the door for his gauntleted hand; and now pulling therewith sturdily, he so cracked, and ripped, and tore all asunder, that the noise of the dry and hollow-sounding wood alarumed and reverberated throughout the forest.'

At the termination of this sentence I started and, for a moment, paused; for it appeared to me (although I at once concluded that my excited fancy had deceived me) – it appeared to me that, from some very remote portion of the mansion, there came, indistinctly to my ears, what might have been, in its exact similarity of character, the echo (but a stifled and dull one certainly) of the very cracking and ripping sound which Sir Launcelot had so particularly described. It was, beyond doubt, the coincidence alone which had arrested my attention; for, amid the rattling of the sashes of the casements, and the ordinary commingled noises of the still increasing storm, the sound, in itself, had nothing, surely, which should have interested or disturbed me. I continued the story:

'But the good champion Ethelred, now entering within the door, was sore enraged and amazed to perceive no signal of the maliceful hermit; but, in the stead thereof, a dragon of a scaly and prodigious demeanor, and of a fiery tongue, which sate in guard before a palace of gold, with a floor of silver; and upon the wall there hung a shield of shining brass with this legend enwritten –

Who entereth herein, a conqueror hath bin;
Who slayeth the dragon, the shield he shall win.

And Ethelred uplifted his mace, and struck upon the head of the dragon, which fell before him, and gave up his pesty breath, with a shriek so horrid and harsh, and withal so piercing, that Ethelred had fain to close his ears with his hands against the dreadful noise of it, the like whereof was never before heard.'

Here again I paused abruptly, and now with a feeling of wild amazement – for there could be no doubt whatever that, in this instance, I did actually hear (although from what direction it proceeded I found it impossible to say) a low and apparently distant, but harsh, protracted, and most unusual screaming or grating sound – the exact counterpart of what my fancy had already conjured up for the dragon's unnatural shriek as described by the romancer.

Oppressed, as I certainly was, upon the occurrence of this second and most extraordinary coincidence, by a thousand conflicting sensations, in which wonder and extreme terror were predominant, I still retained sufficient presence of mind to avoid exciting, by any observation, the sensitive nervousness of my companion. I was by no means certain that he had noticed the sounds in question; although, assuredly, a strange alteration had, during the last few minutes, taken place in his demeanor. From a position fronting my own, he had gradually brought round his chair, so as to sit with his face to the door of the chamber; and thus I could but partially perceive his features, although I saw that his lips trembled as if he were murmuring inaudibly. His head had dropped upon his breast – yet I knew that he was not asleep, from the wide and rigid opening of the eye as I caught a glance of it in profile. The motion of his body, too, was at variance with this idea – for he rocked from side to side with a gentle yet constant and uniform sway. Having rapidly taken notice of all this, I resumed the narration of Sir Launcelot, which thus proceeded:

'And now, the champion, having escaped from the terrible fury of the dragon, bethinking himself of the brazen shield, and of the breaking up of the enchantment which was upon it, removed the carcass from out of the way before him, and approached valorously over the silver pavement of the castle to where the shield was upon the wall; which in sooth tarried not for his full coming, but fell down at his feet upon the silver floor, with a mighty great and terrible ringing sound.'

No sooner had these syllables passed my lips, than – as if a shield of brass had indeed, at the moment, fallen heavily upon a floor of silver – I became aware of a distinct, hollow, metallic, and clangorous, yet apparently muffled, reverberation.

Completely unnerved, I leaped to my feet; but the measured rocking movement of Usher was undisturbed. I rushed to the chair in which he sat. His eyes were bent fixedly before him, and throughout his whole countenance there reigned a stony rigidity. But, as I placed my hand upon his shoulder, there came a strong shudder over his whole person; a sickly smile quivered about his lips; and I saw that he spoke in a low, hurried, and gibbering murmur, as if unconscious of my presence. Bending closely over him, I at length drank in the hideous import of his words.

'Now hear it? – yes, I hear it, and *have* heard it. Long – long– long – many minutes, many hours, many days, have I heard it – yet I dared not – oh, pity me, miserable wretch that I am! – I dared not – I *dared* not speak! *We have put her living in the tomb!* Said I not that my senses were acute? I *now* tell you that I heard her first feeble movements in the hollow coffin. I heard them – many, many days ago – yet I dared not – *I dared not speak!* And now – tonight – Ethelred – ha! ha! – the breaking of the hermit's door, and the death-cry of the dragon, and the clangor of the shield – say, rather, the rending of her coffin, and the grating of the iron hinges of her prison, and her struggles within the coppered archway of the vault! Oh! whither shall I fly? Will she not be here anon? Is she not hurrying to upbraid me for my haste? Have I not heard her footstep on the stair? Do I not distinguish that heavy and horrible beating of her heart? Madman!' – here he sprang furiously to his feet, and shrieked out his syllables, as if in the effort he were giving up his soul – '*Madman! I tell you that she now stands without the door!*'

As if in the superhuman energy of his endurance there had been found the potency of a spell, the huge antique panels to which the speaker pointed threw slowly back, upon the instant, their ponderous and ebony jaws. It was the work of the rushing gust – but then without those doors there *did* stand the lofty and enshrouded figure of the lady Madeline of Usher. There was blood upon her white robes, and the evidence of some bitter struggle upon every portion of her emaciated frame. For a moment she remained trembling and reeling to and fro upon the threshold – then, with a low moaning cry, fell heavily inward upon the person of her brother, and in her violent and now final death-agonies, bore him to the floor a corpse, and a victim to the terrors he had anticipated.

From that chamber, and from that mansion, I fled aghast. The storm was still abroad in all its wrath as I found myself crossing the old causeway. Suddenly there shot along the path a wild light, and I turned to see whence a gleam so unusual could have issued; for the vast house and its shadows were alone behind me. The radiance was that of the full, setting, and blood-red moon, which now shone vividly through that once barely discernible fissure, of which I have before spoken as extending from the roof of the building, in a zigzag direction, to the base. While I gazed, this fissure rapidly widened – there came a fierce breath of the whirlwind – the entire orb of the satellite burst at once upon my sight – my brain reeled as I saw the mighty walls rushing asunder – there was a long tumultuous shouting sound like the voice of a thousand waters – and the deep and dank tarn at my feet closed sullenly and silently over the fragments of the '*House of Usher*'.

The Oval Portrait

The château into which my valet had ventured to
make forcible entrance, rather than permit me, in
my desperately wounded condition, to pass a night
in the open air, was one of those piles of commingled gloom and grandeur which have so long
frowned among the Apennines, not less in fact
than in the fancy of Mrs Radcliffe. To all appearance it had been temporarily and very lately abandoned. We established ourselves in one of the
smallest and least sumptuously furnished apartments. It lay in a remote turret of the building.
Its decorations were rich, yet tattered and antique.
Its walls were hung with tapestry and bedecked
with manifold and multiform armorial trophies,
together with an unusually great number of very
spirited modern paintings in frames of rich golden
arabesque. In these paintings, which depended
from the walls not only in their main surfaces, but
in very many nooks which the bizarre architecture
of the château rendered necessary – in these paintings my incipient delirium, perhaps, had caused
me to take deep interest; so that I bade Pedro to
close the heavy shutters of the room – since it was

already night – to light the tongues of a tall candelabrum which stood by the head of my bed, and to throw open far and wide the fringed curtains of black velvet which enveloped the bed itself. I wished all this done that I might resign myself, if not to sleep, at least alternately to the contemplation of these pictures, and the perusal of a small volume which had been found upon the pillow, and which purported to criticize and describe them.

Long, long I read – and devoutly, devoutly I gazed. Rapidly and gloriously the hours flew by and the deep midnight came. The position of the candelabrum displeased me, and outreaching my hand with difficulty, rather than disturb my slumbering valet, I placed it so as to throw its rays more fully upon the book.

But the action produced an effect altogether unanticipated. The rays of the numerous candles (for there were many) now fell within a niche of the room which had hitherto been thrown into deep shade by one of the bedposts. I thus saw in vivid light a picture all unnoticed before. It was the portrait of a young girl just ripening into womanhood. I glanced at the painting hurriedly, and then closed my eyes. Why I did this was not at first apparent even to my own perception. But while my lids remained thus shut, I ran over in mind my reason for so shutting them. It was an impulsive movement to gain time for thought – to make sure that my vision had not deceived me – to calm and subdue my fancy for a more sober and more certain gaze. In a very few moments I again looked fixedly at the painting.

That I now saw aright I could not and would not doubt; for the first flashing of the candles upon that canvas had seemed to dissipate the dreamy stupor which was stealing over my senses, and to startle me at once into waking life.

The portrait, I have already said, was that of a young girl. It was a mere head and shoulders, done in what is technically termed a *vignette* manner; much in the style of the favorite heads of Sully. The arms, the bosom, and even the ends of the radiant hair melted imperceptibly into the vague yet deep shadow which formed the background of the whole. The frame was oval, richly gilded and filigreed in *Moresque*. As a thing of art nothing could be more admirable than the painting itself. But it could have been neither the execution of the work, nor the immortal beauty of the countenance, which had so suddenly and so vehemently moved me. Least of all, could it have been that my fancy, shaken from its half slumber, had mistaken the head for that of a living person. I saw at once that the peculiarities of the design, of the *vignetting*, and of the frame, must have instantly dispelled such idea – must have prevented even its momentary entertainment. Thinking earnestly upon these points, I remained, for an hour perhaps, half sitting, half reclining, with my vision riveted upon the portrait. At length, satisfied with the true secret of its effect, I fell back within the bed. I had found the spell of the picture in an absolute *life-likeliness* of expression, which, at first startling, finally confounded, subdued, and appalled me. With deep and reverent awe I replaced the candelabrum in its former position. The cause of my deep agitation being thus shut from view, I sought eagerly the volume which discussed the paintings and their histories. Turning to the number which designated the oval portrait, I there read the vague and quaint words which follow:

'She was a maiden of rarest beauty, and not more lovely than full of glee. And evil was the hour when she saw, and loved, and wedded the painter. He, passionate, studious, austere, and having already a bride in his Art: she a maiden of rarest beauty, and not more lovely than full of glee; all light and smiles, and frolicsome as the young fawn; loving and cherishing all things; hating only the Art which was her rival; dreading only the pallet and brushes and other untoward instruments which deprived her of the countenance of her lover. It was thus a terrible thing for this lady to hear the painter speak of his desire to portray even his young bride. But she was humble and obedient, and sat meekly for many weeks in the dark high turret-chamber where the light dripped upon the pale canvas only from overhead. But he, the painter, took glory in his work, which went on from hour to hour, and from day to day. And he was a passionate, and wild, and moody man, who became lost in reveries; so that he *would* not see that the light which fell so ghastly in that lone turret withered the health and the spirits of his bride, who pined visibly to all but him. Yet she smiled on and still on, uncomplainingly, because she saw that the painter (who had high renown) took a fervid and burning pleasure in his task, and wrought day and night to depict her who so loved him, yet who grew daily more dispirited and weak. And in sooth some who beheld the portrait spoke of its resemblance in low words, as of a mighty marvel, and a proof not less of the power of the painter than of his deep love for her whom he depicted so surpassingly well. But at length, as the labor drew nearer to its conclusion, there were admitted none into the turret; for the painter had grown wild with the ardor of his work, and turned his eyes from the canvas rarely, even to regard the countenance of his wife. And he *would* not see that the tints which he spread upon the canvas were drawn from the cheeks of her who sat beside him. And when many weeks had passed, and but little remained to do, save one brush upon the mouth and one tint upon the eye, the spirit of the lady again flickered up as the flame within the socket of the lamp. And then the brush was given, and then the tint was placed; and, for one moment, the painter stood entranced before the work which he had wrought; but in the next, while he yet gazed, he grew tremulous and very pallid, and aghast, and crying with a loud voice, "This is indeed *Life* itself!" turned suddenly to regard his beloved: *She was dead!'*

MS Found in a Bottle

Qui n'a plus qu'un moment à vivre
N'a plus rien à dissimuler.

Quinault – Atys

Of my country and of my family I have little to say. Ill usage and length of years have driven me from the one, and estranged me from the other. Hereditary wealth afforded me an education of no common order, and a contemplative turn of mind enabled me to methodize the stories which early study diligently garnered up. Beyond all things, the works of the German moralists gave me great delight; not from my ill-advised admiration of their eloquent madness, but from the ease with which my habits of rigid thoughts enabled me to detect their falsities. I have often been reproached with the aridity of my genius; a deficiency of imagination has been imputed to me as a crime; and the Pyrrhonism of my opinions has at all times rendered me notorious. Indeed, a strong relish for physical philosophy has, I fear, tinctured my mind with a very common error of this age – I mean the habit of referring occurrences, even the least susceptible of such reference, to the principles of that science. Upon the whole, no person could be less liable than myself to be led away from the severe precincts of truth by the *ignes fatui* of superstition. I have thought proper to premise thus much, lest the incredible tale I have to tell should be considered rather the raving of a crude imagination, than the positive experience of a mind to which the reveries of fancy have been a dead letter and a nullity.

After many years spent in foreign travel, I sailed in the year 18—, from the port of Batavia, in the rich and populous island of Java, on a voyage to the Archipelago Islands. I went as passenger – having no other inducement than a kind of nervous restlessness which haunted me as a fiend.

Our vessel was a beautiful ship of about four hundred tons, copper-fastened, and built at Bombay of Malabar teak. She was freighted with cotton-wool and oil, from the Lachadive Islands. We had also on board coir, jaggeree, ghee, coconuts, and a few cases of opium. The stowage was clumsily done, and the vessel consequently crank.

We got under way with a mere breath of wind, and for many days stood along the eastern coast of Java, without any other incident to beguile the monotony of our course than the occasional meeting with some of the small grabs of the Archipelago to which we were bound.

One evening, leaning over the taffrail, I

observed a very singular isolated cloud, to the NW. It was remarkable, as well from its color as from its being the first we had seen since our departure from Batavia. I watched it attentively until sunset, when it spread all at once to the eastward and westward, girting in the horizon with a narrow strip of vapor, and looking like a long line of low beach. My notice was soon afterward attracted by the dusky-red appearance of the moon, and the peculiar character of the sea. The latter was undergoing a rapid change, and the water seemed more than usually transparent. Although I could distinctly see the bottom, yet, heaving the lead, I found the ship in fifteen fathoms. The air now became intolerably hot, and was loaded with spiral exhalations similar to those arising from heated iron. As night came on, every breath of wind died away, and a more entire calm it is impossible to conceive. The flame of a candle burned upon the poop without the least perceptible motion, and a long hair, held between the finger and thumb, hung without the possibility of detecting a vibration. However, as the captain said he could perceive no indication of danger, and as we were drifting in bodily to shore, he ordered the sails to be furled, and the anchor let go. No watch was set, and the crew, consisting principally of Malays, stretched themselves deliberately upon deck. I went below – not without a full presentiment of evil. Indeed, every appearance warranted me in apprehending a simoon. I told the captain of my fears; but he paid no attention to what I said, and left me without deigning to give a reply. My uneasiness, however, prevented me from sleeping, and about midnight I went upon deck. As I placed my foot upon the upper step of the companion-ladder, I was startled by a loud, humming noise, like that occasioned by the rapid revolution of a mill-wheel, and before I could ascertain its meaning, I found the ship quivering to its centre. In the next instant a wilderness of foam hurled us upon our beam-ends, and, rushing over us fore and aft, swept the entire decks from stem to stern.

The extreme fury of the blast proved, in a great measure, the salvation of the ship. Although completely waterlogged, yet, as her masts had gone by the board, she rose, after a minute, heavily from the sea, and, staggering awhile beneath the immense pressure of the tempest, finally righted.

By what miracle I escaped destruction, it is impossible to say. Stunned by the shock of the water, I found myself, upon recovery, jammed in between the stern-post and rudder. With great difficulty I regained my feet, and looking dizzily around, was at first struck with the idea of our being among breakers; so terrific, beyond the wildest imagination, was the whirlpool of mountainous and foaming ocean within which we were engulfed. After a while I heard the voice of an old Swede, who had shipped with us at the moment of leaving port. I hallooed to him with all my strength, and presently he came reeling aft. We soon discovered that we were the sole survivors of the accident. All on deck, with the exception of ourselves, had been swept overboard; the captain and mates must have perished while they slept, for the cabins were deluged with water. Without assistance we could expect to do little for the security of the ship, and our exertions were at first paralysed by the momentary expectation of going down. Our cable had, of course, parted like pack-thread, at the first breath of the hurricane, or we should have been instantaneously over-whelmed. We scudded with frightful velocity before the sea, and the water made clear breaches over us. The framework of our stern was shattered excessively, and, in almost every respect, we had received considerable injury; but to our extreme joy we found the pumps unchoked, and that we had made no great shifting of our ballast. The main fury of the blast had already blown over, and we apprehended little danger from the viol-ence of the wind; but we looked forward to its total cessation with dismay; well believing, that in our shattered condition, we should inevitably perish in the tremendous swell which would ensue. But this very just apprehension seemed by no means likely to be soon verified. For five entire days and nights – during which our only subsist-ence was a small quantity of jaggeree, procured with great difficulty from the forecastle – the hulk flew at a rate defying computation, before rapidly succeeding flaws of wind, which, without equalling the first violence of the simoon, were still more terrific than any tempest I had before encountered. Our course for the first four days was, with trifling variations, SE and by S; and we must have run down the coast of New Holland. On the fifth day the cold became extreme, although the wind had hauled round a point more to the northward. The sun arose with a sickly yellow lustre, and clambered a very few degrees above the horizon – emitting no decisive light. There were no clouds apparent, yet the wind was upon the increase, and blew with a fitful and unsteady fury. About noon, as nearly as we could guess, our attention was again arrested by the appearance of the sun. It gave out no light, properly so called, but a dull and sullen glow without reflection, as if all its rays were polarized. Just before sinking within the turgid sea, its central fires suddenly went out, as if hurriedly extinguished by some unaccountable power. It was a dim, silver-like rim, alone, as it rushed down the unfathomable ocean.

We waited in vain for the arrival of the sixth day – that day to me has not yet arrived – to the Swede never did arrive. Thenceforward we were enshrouded in pitchy darkness, so that we could not have seen an object at twenty paces from the ship. Eternal night continued to envelop us, all unrelieved by the phosphoric sea-brilliancy to which we had been accustomed in the tropics. We observed, too, that, although the tempest continued to rage with unabated violence, there was no longer to be discovered the usual appearance of surf, or foam, which had hitherto attended us. All around were horror, and thick gloom, and a black sweltering desert of ebony. Superstitious terror crept by degrees into the spirit of the old Swede, and my own soul was wrapt in silent wonder. We neglected all care of the ship, as worse than useless, and securing ourselves as well as possible to the stump of the mizen-mast, looked out bitterly into the world of ocean. We had no means of calculating time, nor could we form any guess of our situation. We were, however, well aware of having made farther to the southward than any previous navigators, and felt great amazement at not meeting with the usual impediments of ice. In the mean time every moment threatened to be our last – every mountainous billow hurried to overwhelm us. The swell surpassed anything I had imagined possible, and that we were not instantly buried is a miracle. My companion spoke of the lightness of our cargo, and reminded me of the excellent qualities of our ship; but I could not help feeling the utter hopelessness of hope itself, and prepared myself gloomily for that death which I thought nothing could defer beyond an hour, as, with every knot of way the ship made, the swelling of the black stupendous seas became more dismally appalling. At times we gasped for breath at an elevation beyond the albatross – at times became dizzy with the velocity of our descent into some watery hell, where the air grew stagnant, and no sound disturbed the slumbers of the kraken.

We were at the bottom of one of these abysses, when a quick scream from my companion broke fearfully upon the night. 'See! see!' cried he, shrieking in my ears, 'Almighty God! see! see!' As he spoke I became aware of a dull sullen glare of red light which streamed down the sides of the vast chasm where we lay, and threw a fitful brilliancy upon our deck. Casting my eyes upwards, I beheld a spectacle which froze the current of my blood. At a terrific height directly above us, and upon the very verge of the precipitous descent, hovered a gigantic ship of perhaps four thousand tons. Although upreared upon the summit of a wave more than a hundred times her own altitude, her apparent size still exceeded that of any ship of the line or East Indiaman in existence. Her huge hull was of a deep dingy black, unrelieved by any of the customary carvings of a ship. A single row of brass cannon protruded from her open ports, and dashed from the polished surfaces the fires of innumerable battle-lanterns which swung to and fro about her rigging. But what mainly inspired us with horror and astonishment, was that she bore up under a press of sail in the very teeth of that supernatural sea, and of that ungovernable hurricane. When we first discovered her, her bows were alone to be seen, as she rose slowly from the dim and horrible gulf beyond her. For a moment of intense terror she paused upon the giddy

pinnacle as if in contemplation of her own sublim-
ity, then trembled, and tottered, and – came down.

At this instant, I know not what sudden self-
possession came over my spirit. Staggering as far
aft as I could, I awaited fearlessly the ruin that
was to overwhelm. Our own vessel was at length
ceasing from her struggles, and sinking with her
head to the sea. The shock of the descending mass
struck her, consequently, in that portion of her
frame which was nearly under water, and the
inevitable result was to hurl me, with irresistible
violence, upon the rigging of the stranger.

As I fell, the ship hove in stays, and went
about; and to the confusion ensuing I attributed
my escape from the notice of the crew. With little
difficulty I made my way, unperceived, to the
main hatchway, which was partially open, and
soon found an opportunity of secreting myself in
the hold. Why I did so I can hardly tell. An
indefinite sense of awe, which at first sight of the
navigators of the ship had taken hold of my mind,
was perhaps the principle of my concealment. I
was unwilling to trust myself with a race of people
who had offered, to the cursory glance I had
taken, so many points of vague novelty, doubt,
and apprehension. I therefore thought proper to
contrive a hiding-place in the hold. This I did by
removing a small portion of the shifting-boards,
in such a manner as to afford me a convenient
retreat between the huge timbers of the ship.

I had scarcely completed my work, when a

footstep in the hold forced me to make use of it. A man passed by my place of concealment with a feeble and unsteady gait. I could not see his face, but had an opportunity of observing his general appearance. There was about it an evidence of great age and infirmity. His knees tottered beneath a load of years, and his entire frame quivered under the burden. He muttered to himself, in a low broken tone, some words of a language which I could not understand, and groped in a corner among a pile of singular-looking instruments, and decayed charts of navigation. His manner was a wild mixture of the peevishness of second child-hood, and the solemn dignity of a God. He at length went on deck, and I saw him no more.

A feeling, for which I have no name, has taken possession of my soul – a sensation which will admit of no analysis, to which the lessons of bygone time are inadequate, and for which I fear futurity itself will offer me no key. To a mind constituted like my own, the latter consideration is an evil. I shall never – I know that I shall never – be satisfied with regard to the nature of my conceptions. Yet it is not wonderful that these conceptions are indefinite, since they have their origin in sources so utterly novel. A new sense – a new entity is added to my soul.

It is long since I first trod the deck of this terrible ship, and the rays of my destiny are, I think, gathering to a focus. Incomprehensible men! Wrapped up in meditations of a kind which I cannot divine, they pass me by unnoticed. Concealment is utter folly on my part, for the people *will not* see. It is but just now that I passed directly before the eyes of the mate; it was no long while ago that I ventured into the captain's own private cabin, and took thence the materials with which I write, and have written. I shall from time to time continue this journal. It is true that I may not find an opportunity of transmitting it to the world, but I will not fail to make the endeavor. At the last moment I will enclose the MS in a bottle, and cast it within the sea.

An incident has occurred which has given me new room for meditation. Are such things the operation of ungoverned chance? I had ventured upon deck and thrown myself down, without attracting any notice, among a pile of ratlin-stuff and old sails, in the bottom of the yawl. While musing upon the singularity of my fate, I unwittingly daubed with a tar-brush the edges of a neatly folded studding-sail which lay near me on a barrel. The studding-sail is now bent upon the ship, and the thoughtless touches of the brush are spread out into the word DISCOVERY.

I have made my observations lately upon the structure of the vessel. Although well armed, she is not, I think, a ship of war. Her rigging, build, and general equipment, all negative a supposition of this kind. What she *is not*, I can easily perceive; what she *is*, I fear it is impossible to say. I know not how it is, but in scrutinizing her strange model and singular cast of spars, her huge size and overgrown suits of canvas, her severely simple bow and antiquated stern, there will occasionally flash across my mind a sensation of familiar things, and there is always mixed up with such indistinct shadows of recollection, an unaccountable memory of old foreign chronicles and ages long ago.

I have been looking at the timbers of the ship. She is built of a material to which I am a stranger. There is a peculiar character about the wood which strikes me as rendering it unfit for the purpose to which it has been applied. I mean its extreme *porousness*, considered independently of the worm-eaten condition which is a consequence of navigation in these seas, and apart from the rottenness attendant upon age. It will appear perhaps an observation somewhat over-curious, but this would have every characteristic of Spanish oak, if Spanish oak were distended by any unnatural means.

In reading the above sentence, a curious apothegm of an old weather-beaten Dutch navigator comes full upon my recollection. 'It is as sure', he was wont to say, when any doubt was entertained of his veracity, 'as sure as there is a sea where the ship itself will grow in bulk like the living body of the seaman.'

About an hour ago, I made bold to trust myself among a group of the crew. They paid me no manner of attention, and, although I stood in the very midst of them all, seemed utterly unconscious of my presence. Like the one I had at first seen in the hold, they all bore about them the marks of a hoary old age. Their knees trembled with infirmity; their shoulders were bent double with decrepitude; their shrivelled skins rattled in the wind; their voices were low, tremulous, and broken; their eyes glistened with the rheum of years; and their gray hairs streamed terribly in the tempest. Around them, on every part of the deck, lay scattered mathematical instruments of the most quaint and obsolete construction.

I mentioned, some time ago, the bending of a studding-sail. From that period, the ship, being thrown dead off the wind, has continued her terrific course due south, with every rag of canvas packed upon her, from her truck to her lower studding-sail booms, and rolling every moment her top-gallant yard-arms into the most appalling hell of water which it can enter into the mind of man to imagine. I have just left the deck, where I find it impossible to maintain a footing, although the crew seem to experience little inconvenience. It appears to me a miracle of miracles that our enormous bulk is not swallowed up at once and for ever. We are surely doomed to hover continually upon the brink of eternity, without taking a final plunge into the abyss. From billows a thousand times more stupendous than any I have ever seen, we glide away with the facility of the arrowy seagull; and the colossal waters rear their heads above us like demons of the deep, but like demons confined to simple threats, and forbidden to destroy. I am led to attribute these frequent escapes to the only natural cause which can account for such effect. I must suppose the ship to be within the influence of some strong current, or impetuous undertow.

I have seen the captain face to face, and in his own cabin – but, as I expected, he paid me no attention. Although in his appearance there is, to a casual observer, nothing which might bespeak him more or less than man, still, a feeling of irrepressible reverence and awe mingled with the sensation of wonder with which I regarded him. In stature, he is nearly my own height; that is, about five feet eight inches. He is of a well-knit and compact frame of body, neither robust nor remarkable otherwise. But it is the singularity of the expression which reigns upon the face – it is the intense, the wonderful, the thrilling evidence of old age so utter, so extreme, which excites within my spirit a sense – a sentiment ineffable. His forehead, although little wrinkled, seems to bear upon it the stamp of a myriad of years. His gray hairs are records of the past, and his grayer eyes are sybils of the future. The cabin floor was thickly strewn with strange, iron-clasped folios, and mouldering instruments of science, and obsolete long-forgotten charts. His head was bowed down upon his hands, and he pored, with a fiery, unquiet eye, over a paper which I took to be a commission, and which, at all events, bore the signature of a monarch. He murmured to himself – as did the first seaman whom I saw in the hold – some low peevish syllables of a foreign tongue; and although the speaker was close at my elbow, his voice seemed to reach my ears from the distance of a mile.

The ship and all in it are imbued with the spirit of Eld. The crew glide to and fro like the ghosts of buried centuries; their eyes have an eager and uneasy meaning; and when their fingers fall athwart my path in the wild glare of the battle-lanterns, I feel as I have never felt before, although I have been all my life a dealer in antiquities, and have imbibed the shadows of fallen columns at Balbec, and Tadmor, and Persepolics, until my very soul has become a ruin.

When I look around me, I feel ashamed of my former apprehension. If I trembled at the blast which has hitherto attended us, shall I not stand aghast at a warring of wind and ocean, to convey any idea of which, the words tornado and simoon are trivial and ineffective? All in the immediate vicinity of the ship is the blackness of eternal light, and a chaos of foamless water; but, about a league on either side of us, may be seen, indistinctly and at intervals, stupendous ramparts of ice, towering away into the desolate sky, and looking like the walls of the universe.

As I imagined, the ship proves to be in a current — if that appellation can properly be given to a tide which, howling and shrieking by the white ice, thunders on to the southward with a velocity like the headlong dashing of a cataract.

To conceive the horror of my sensations is, I presume, utterly impossible; yet a curiosity to penetrate the mysteries of these awful regions, predominates even over my despair, and will reconcile me to the most hideous aspect of death. It is evident that we are hurrying onward to some exciting knowledge — some never-to-be-imparted secret, whose attainment is destruction. Perhaps this current leads us to the southern pole itself. It must be confessed that a supposition apparently so wild has every probability in its favor.

The crew pace the deck with unquiet and tremulous step; but there is upon their countenance an expression more of the eagerness of hope than of the apathy of despair.

In the mean time the wind is still in our poop, and, as we carry a crowd of canvas, the ship is at times lifted bodily from out the sea! Oh, horror upon horror! – the ice opens suddenly to the right, and to the left, and we are whirling dizzily, in immense concentric circles, round and round the borders of a gigantic amphitheatre, the summit of whose walls is lost in the darkness and the distance. But little time will be left me to ponder upon my destiny! The circles rapidly grow small – we are plunging madly within the grasp of the whirlpool – and amid a roaring, and bellowing, and thundering of ocean and tempest, the ship is quivering – oh God! and – going down!

Note The 'MS Found in a Bottle', was originally published in 1831, and it was not until many years afterwards that I became acquainted with the maps of Mercator, in which the ocean is represented as rushing, by four mouths, into the (northern) Polar Gulf, to be absorbed into the bowels of the earth, the Pole itself being represented by a black rock, towering to a prodigious height.

A Descent into the Maelström

The ways of God in Nature, as in Providence, are not as *our* ways; nor are the models that we frame in any way commensurate to the vastness, profundity, and unsearchableness of His works, *which have a depth in them greater than the well of Dermocritus.*

— Joseph Glanville

We had now reached the summit of the loftiest crag. For some minutes the old man seemed too much exhausted to speak.

'Not long ago,' said he at length, 'and I could have guided you on this route as well as the youngest of my sons; but, about three years past, there happened to me an event such as never happened before to mortal man – or at least such as no man ever survived to tell of – and the six hours of deadly terror which I then endured have broken me up body and soul. You suppose me a *very* old man – but I am not. It took less than a single day to change these hairs from a jetty black to white, to weaken my limbs, and to unstring my nerves, so that I tremble at the least exertion, and am frightened at a shadow. Do you know I can scarcely look over this little cliff without getting giddy?'

The 'little cliff', upon whose edge he had so carelessly thrown himself down to rest that the weightier portion of his body hung over it, while he was only kept from falling by the tenure of his elbow on its extreme and slippery edge – this 'little cliff' arose, a sheer unobstructed precipice of black shining rock, some fifteen or sixteen hundred feet from the world of crags beneath us. Nothing would have tempted me to be within half a dozen yards of its brink. In truth so deeply was I excited by the perilous position of my companion, that I fell at full length upon the ground, clung to the shrubs around me, and dared not even glance upward at the sky – while I struggled in vain to divest myself of the idea that the very foundations of the mountain were in danger from the fury of the winds. It was long before I could reason myself into sufficient courage to sit up and look out into the distance.

'You must get over these fancies,' said the guide, 'for I have brought you here that you might have the best possible view of the scene of that event I mentioned – and to tell you the whole story with the spot just under your eye.

'We are now,' he continued, in that particularizing manner which distinguished him – 'we are now close upon the Norwegian coast – in the sixty-eighth degree of latitude – in the great province of Nordland – and in the dreary district of Lofoden. The mountain upon whose top we sit is Helseggen, the Cloudy. Now raise yourself up a little higher – hold on to the grass if you feel giddy – so – and look out, beyond the belt of vapor beneath us, into the sea.'

I looked dizzily, and beheld a wide expanse of ocean, whose waters wore so inky a hue as to bring at once to my mind the Nubian geographer's account of the *Mare Tenebrarum*. A panorama more deplorably desolate no human imagination can conceive. To the right and left, as far as the eye could reach, there lay outstretched, like ramparts of the world, lines of horridly black and beetling cliff, whose character of gloom was but the more forcibly illustrated by the surf which reared high up against it its white and ghastly crest, howling and shrieking for ever. Just opposite the promontory upon whose apex we were placed, and at a distance of some five or six miles out at sea, there was visible a small, bleak-looking island; or, more properly, its position was discernible through the wilderness of surge in which it was enveloped. About two miles nearer the land, arose another of smaller size, hideously craggy and barren, and encompassed at various intervals by a cluster of dark rocks.

The appearance of the ocean, in the space between the more distant island and the shore, had something very unusual about it. Although, at the time, so strong a gale was blowing landward that a brig in the remote offing lay to under a double-reefed trysail, and constantly plunged her whole hull out of sight, still there was here nothing like a regular swell, but only a short, quick, angry cross dashing of water in every direction – as well in the teeth of the wind as otherwise. Of foam there was little except in the immediate vicinity of the rocks.

'The island in the distance,' resumed the old man, 'is called by the Norwegians Vurrgh. The one midway is Moskoe. That a mile to the north-ward is Ambaaren. Yonder are Islesen, Hotholm, Keildhelm, Suarven, and Buckholm. Further off – between Moskoe and Vurrgh – are Otterholm, Flimen, Sandflesen, and Skarholm. These are the true names of the places – but why it has been thought necessary to name them at all, is more than either you or I can understand. Do you hear any thing? Do you see any change in the water?'

We had now been about ten minutes upon the top of Helseggen, to which we had ascended from the interior of Lofoden, so that we had caught no glimpse of the sea until it had burst upon us from the summit. As the old man spoke, I became aware of a loud and gradually increasing sound, like the moaning of a vast herd of buffaloes upon an American prairie; and at the same moment I perceived that what seamen term the *chopping* character of the ocean beneath us, was rapidly changing into a current which set to the eastward. Even while I gazed, this current acquired a mon-strous velocity. Each moment added to its speed –

to its headlong impetuosity. In five minutes the whole sea, as far as Vurrgh, was lashed into ungovernable fury; but it was between Moskoe and the coast that the main uproar held its sway. Here the vast bed of the waters, seamed and scarred into a thousand conflicting channels, burst suddenly into frenzied convulsion – heaving, boiling, hissing – gyrating in gigantic and innumerable vortices, and all whirling and plunging on to the eastward with a rapidity which water never elsewhere assumes, except in precipitous descents.

In a few minutes more, there came over the scene another radical alteration. The general surface grew somewhat more smooth, and the whirlpools, one by one, disappeared, while prodigious streaks of foam became apparent where none had been seen before. These streaks, at length, spreading out to a great distance, and entering into combination, took unto themselves the gyratory motion of the subsided vortices, and seemed to form the germ of another more vast. Suddenly – very suddenly – this assumed a distinct and definite existence, in a circle of more than a mile in diameter. The edge of the whirl was represented by a broad belt of gleaming spray; but no particle of this slipped into the mouth of the terrific funnel, whose interior, as far as the eye could fathom it, was a smooth, shining, and jet-black wall of water, inclined to the horizon at an angle of some forty-five degrees, speeding dizzily round and round with a swaying and sweltering motion, and sending forth to the winds an appalling voice, half shriek, half roar, such as not even the mighty cataract of Niagara ever lifts up in its agony to Heaven.

The mountain trembled to its very base, and the rock rocked. I threw myself upon my face, and clung to the scant herbage in an excess of nervous agitation.

'This,' said I at length, to the old man – 'this *can* be nothing else than the great whirlpool of the Maelström.'

'So it is sometimes termed,' said he. 'We Norwegians call it the Moskoe-ström, from the island of Moskoe in the midway.'

The ordinary account of this vortex had by no means prepared me for what I saw. That of Jonas Ramus, which is perhaps the most circumstantial of any, cannot impart the faintest conception either of the magnificence, or of the horror of the scene – or of the wild bewildering sense of *the novel* which confounds the beholder. I am not sure from what point of view the writer in question surveyed it, nor at what time; but it could neither have been from the summit of Helseggen, nor during a storm. There are some passages of his description, nevertheless, which may be quoted for their details, although their effect is exceedingly feeble in conveying an impression of the spectacle.

'Between Lofoden and Moskoe,' he says, 'the depth of the water is between thirty-six and forty fathoms; but on the other side, toward Ver (Vurrgh) this depth decreases so as not to afford a convenient passage for a vessel, without the risk of splitting on the rocks, which happens even in the calmest weather. When it is flood, the stream runs up the country between Lofoden and Moskoe with a boisterous rapidity; but the roar of its impetuous ebb to the sea is scarce equalled by the loudest and most dreadful cataracts; the noise being heard several leagues off, and the vortices or pits are of such an extent and depth, that if a ship comes within its attraction, it is inevitably absorbed and carried down to the bottom, and there beat to pieces against the rocks; and when the water relaxes, the fragments thereof are thrown up again. But these intervals of tranquillity are only at the turn of the ebb and flood, and in calm weather, and last but a quarter of an hour, its violence gradually returning. When the stream is most boisterous, and its fury heightened by a storm, it is dangerous to come within a Norway mile of it. Boats, yachts, and ships have been carried away by not guarding against it before they were carried within its reach. It likewise happens frequently, that whales come too near the stream, and are overpowered by its violence; and then it is impossible to describe their howlings and bellowings in their fruitless struggles to disengage themselves. A bear once, attempting to swim from Lofoden to Moskoe, was caught by the stream and borne down, while he roared terribly, so as to be heard on shore. Large stocks of firs and pine trees, after being absorbed by the current, rise again broken and torn to such a degree as if bristles grew upon them. This plainly shows the bottom to consist of craggy rocks, among which they are whirled to and fro. This stream is regulated by the flux and reflux of the sea – it being constantly high and low water every six hours. In the year 1645, early in the morning of Sexagesima Sunday, it raged with such noise and impetuosity that the very stones of the houses on the coast fell to the ground.'

In regard to the depth of the water, I could not see how this could have been ascertained at all in the immediate vicinity of the vortex. The 'forty fathoms' must have reference only to portions of the channel close upon the shore either of Moskoe or Lofoden. The depth in the centre of the Moskoe-ström must be unmeasurably greater; and no better proof of this fact is necessary than can be obtained from even the sidelong glance into the abyss of the whirl which may be had from the highest crag of Helseggen. Looking down from this pinnacle upon the howling Phlegethon below, I could not help smiling at the simplicity with which the honest Jonas Ramus records, as a matter difficult of belief, the anecdotes of the whales and the bears, for it appeared to me, in fact, a self-evident thing, that the largest ships of the line in existence, coming within the influence of that deadly attraction, could resist it as little as a feather the hurricane, and must disappear bodily and at once.

The attempts to account for the phenomenon – some of which, I remember, seemed to me sufficiently plausible in perusal – now wore a very different and unsatisfactory aspect. The idea generally received is that this, as well as three smaller vortices among the Ferroe Islands, 'have no other cause than the collision of waves rising and falling, at flux and reflux, against a ridge of rocks and shelves, which confines the water so that it precipitates itself like a cataract; and thus the higher the flood rises, the deeper must the fall be, and the natural result of all is a whirlpool or vortex, the prodigious suction of which is sufficiently known by lesser experiments.' These are the words of the *Encyclopaedia Britannica*. Kircher and others imagine that in the centre of the channel of the maelström is an abyss penetrating the globe, and issuing in some very remote part – the Gulf of Bothnia being somewhat decidedly named in one instance. This opinion, idle in itself, was the one to which, as I gazed, my imagination most readily assented; and, mentioning it to the guide, I was rather surprised to hear him say that, although it was the view almost universally entertained of the subject by the Norwegians, it nevertheless was not his own. As to the former notion he confessed his inability to comprehend it; and here I agreed with him – for, however conclusive on paper, it becomes altogether unintelligible, and even absurd, amid the thunder of the abyss.

'You have had a good look at the whirl now,' said the old man, 'and if you will creep round this crag, so as to get in its lee, and deaden the roar of the water, I will tell you a story that will convince you I ought to know something of the Moskoe-ström.'

I placed myself as desired, and he proceeded.

'Myself and my two brothers once owned a schooner-rigged smack of about seventy tons burden, with which we were in the habit of fishing among the islands beyond Moskoe, nearly to Vurrgh. In all violent eddies at sea there is good fishing, at proper opportunities, if one has only the courage to attempt it; but among the whole of the Lofoden coastmen, we three were the only ones who made a regular business of going out to the islands, as I tell you. The usual grounds are a great way lower down to the southward. There fish can be got at all hours, without much risk, and therefore these places are preferred. The choice spots over here among the rocks, however, not only yield the finest variety, but in far greater abundance; so that we often got in a single day, what the more timid of the craft could not scrape together in a week. In fact, we made it a matter of desperate speculation – the risk of life standing instead of labor, and courage answering for capital.

'We kept the smack in a cove about five miles higher up the coast than this; and it was our practice, in fine weather, to take advantage of the fifteen minutes' slack to push across the main channel of the Moskoe-ström, far above the pool, and then drop down upon anchorage somewhere near Otterholm, or Sandflesen, where the eddies are not so violent as elsewhere. Here we used to remain until nearly time for slack-water again, when we weighed and made for home. We never set out upon this expedition without a steady side wind for going and coming – one that we felt sure would not fail us before our return – and we seldom made a miscalculation upon this point. Twice, during six years, we were forced to stay all night at anchor on account of a dead calm, which is a rare thing indeed just about here; and once we had to remain on the grounds nearly a week, starving to death, owing to a gale which blew up shortly after our arrival, and made the channel too boisterous to be thought of. Upon this occasion we should have been driven out to sea in spite of everything (for the whirlpools threw us round and round so violently, that, at length, we fouled our anchor and dragged it), if it had not been that we drifted into one of the innumerable cross currents – here today and gone tomorrow – which drove us under the lee of Flimen, where, by good luck, we brought up.

'I could not tell you the twentieth part of the difficulties we encountered "on the ground" – it is a bad spot to be in, even in good weather – but we make shift always to run the gauntlet of the Moskoe-ström itself without accident; although at times my heart has been in my mouth when we happened to be a minute or so behind or before the slack. The wind sometimes was not as strong as we thought it at starting, and then we made rather less way than we could wish, while the current rendered the smack unmanageable. My eldest brother had a son eighteen years old, and I had two stout boys of my own. These would have been of great assistance at such times, in using the sweeps as well as afterward in fishing – but, somehow, although we ran the risk ourselves, we had not the heart to let the young ones get into the danger – for, after all said and done, it *was* a horrible danger, and that is the truth.

'It is now within a few days of three years since what I am going to tell you occurred. It was on the tenth of July, 18—, a day which the people of this part of the world will never forget – for it was one in which blew the most terrible hurricane that ever came out of the heavens. And yet all the morning, and indeed until late in the afternoon, there was a gentle and steady breeze from the southwest, while the sun shone brightly, so that the oldest seaman among us could not have foreseen what was to follow.

'The three of us – my two brothers and myself – had crossed over to the islands about two o'clock p.m., and soon nearly loaded the smack with fine fish, which, we all remarked, were more plenty that day than we had ever known them. It was just seven, *by my watch*, when we weighed and started for home, so as to make the worst of the Ström at slack water, which we knew would be at eight.

'We set out with a fresh wind on our starboard quarter, and for some time spanked along at a great rate, never dreaming of danger, for indeed we saw not the slightest reason to apprehend it. All at once we were taken aback by a breeze from over Helseggen. This was most unusual – something that had never happened to us before – and I began to feel a little uneasy, without exactly knowing why. We put the boat on the wind, but could make no headway at all for the eddies, and I was upon the point of proposing to return to the anchorage, when, looking astern, we saw the whole horizon covered with a singular copper-colored cloud that rose with the most amazing velocity.

'In the mean time the breeze that had headed us off fell away and we were dead becalmed, drifting about in every direction. This state of things, however, did not last long enough to give us time to think about it. In less than a minute the storm was upon us – in less than two the sky was entirely overcast – and what with this and the driving spray, it became suddenly so dark that we could not see each other in the smack.

'Such a hurricane as then blew it is folly to attempt describing. The oldest seaman in Norway never experienced anything like it. We had let our sails go by the run before it cleverly took us; but, at the first puff, both our masts went by the board as if they had been sawed off – the mainmast taking with it my youngest brother, who had lashed himself to it for safety.

'Our boat was the lightest feather of a thing that ever sat upon water. It had a complete flush deck, with only a small hatch near the bow, and this hatch it had always been our custom to batten down when about to cross the Ström, by way of precaution against the chopping seas. But for this circumstance we should have foundered at once – for we lay entirely buried for some moments. How my elder brother escaped destruction I cannot say, for I never had an opportunity of ascertaining. For my part, as soon as I had let the foresail run, I threw myself flat on deck, with my feet against the narrow gunwale of the bow, and with my hands grasping a ring-bolt near the foot of the foremast. It was mere instinct that prompted me to do this – which was undoubtedly the very best thing I could have done – for I was too much flurried to think.

'For some moments we were completely deluged, as I say, and all this time I held my breath, and clung to the bolt. When I could stand it no longer I raised myself upon my knees, still keeping hold with my hands, and thus got my head clear. Presently our little boat gave herself a shake, just as a dog does in coming out of the water, and thus rid herself, in some measure, of the seas. I was now trying to get the better of the stupor that had

come over me, and to collect my senses so as to
see what was to be done, when I felt somebody
grasp my arm. It was my elder brother, and my
heart leaped for joy, for I had made sure that he
was overboard – but the next moment all this joy
was turned into horror – for he put his mouth
close to my ear, and screamed out the word
"*Moskoe-ström!*"

'No one ever will know what my feelings were
at that moment. I shook from head to foot as if I
had had the most violent fit of the ague. I knew
what he meant by that one word well enough – I
knew what he wished to make me understand.
With the wind that now drove us on, we were
bound for the whirl of the Ström, and nothing
could save us!

'You perceive that in crossing the Ström *channel*, we always went a long way up above the
whirl, even in the calmest weather, and then had
to wait and watch carefully for the slack – but
now we were driving right upon the pool itself,
and in such a hurricane as this! "To be sure," I
thought, "we shall get there just about the slack –
there is some little hope in that" – but in the next
moment I cursed myself for being so great a fool
as to dream of hope at all. I knew very well that
we were doomed, had we been ten times a ninety-
gun ship.

'By this time the first fury of the tempest had
spent itself, or perhaps we did not feel it so much,
as we scudded before it, but at all events the seas,

which at first had been kept down by the wind, and lay flat and frothing, now got up into absolute mountains. A singular change, too, had come over the heavens. Around in every direction it was still as black as pitch, but nearly overhead there burst out, all at once, a circular rift of clear sky – as clear as I ever saw – and of a deep bright blue – and through it there blazed forth the full moon with a lustre that I never before knew her to wear. She lit up everything about us with the greatest distinctness – but, oh God, what a scene it was to light up!

'I now made one or two attempts to speak to my brother – but in some manner which I could not understand, the din had so increased that I could not make him hear a single word, although I screamed at the top of my voice in his ear. Presently he shook his head, looking as pale as death, and held up one of his fingers as if to say *"listen!"*

'At first I could not make out what he meant – but soon a hideous thought flashed upon me. I dragged my watch from its fob. It was not going. I glanced at its face by the moonlight, and then burst into tears as I flung it far away into the ocean. *It had run down at seven o'clock! We were behind the time of the slack, and the whirl of the Ström was in full fury!*

'When a boat is well built, properly trimmed, and not deep laden, the waves in a strong gale, when she is going large, seem always to slip from beneath her – which appears strange to a landsman – and this is what is called *riding*, in sea phrase.

'Well, so far we had ridden the swells very cleverly; but presently a gigantic sea happened to take us right under the counter, and bore us with it as it rose – up – up – as if into the sky. I would not have believed that any wave could rise so high. And then down we came with a sweep, a slide, and a plunge that made me feel sick and dizzy, as if I was falling from some lofty mountain-top in a dream. But while we were up I had thrown a quick glance around – and that one glance was all-sufficient. I saw our exact position in an instant. The Moskoe-ström whirlpool was about a quarter of a mile dead ahead – but no more like the everyday Moskoe-ström than the whirl, as you now see it, is like a mill-race. If I had not known where we were, and what we had to expect, I should not have recognized the place at all. As it was, I involuntarily closed my eyes in horror. The lids clenched themselves together as if in a spasm.

'It could not have been more than two minutes afterwards until we suddenly felt the waves subside, and were enveloped in foam. The boat made a sharp half-turn to larboard, and then shot off in its new direction like a thunderbolt. At the same moment the roaring noise of the water was completely drowned in a kind of shrill shriek – such a noise as you might imagine given out by the water-pipes of many thousand steam-vessels letting off their steam all together. We were now in the belt of surf that always surrounds the whirl; and I thought, of course, that another moment would plunge us into the abyss, down which we could only see indistinctly on account of the amazing velocity with which we were borne along. The boat did not seem to sink into the water at all, but to skim like an air-bubble upon the surface of the surge. Her starboard side was next the whirl, and on the larboard arose the world of ocean we had left. It stood like a huge writhing wall between us and the horizon.

'It may appear strange, but now, when we were in the very jaws of the gulf, I felt more composed than when we were only approaching it. Having made up my mind to hope no more, I got rid of a great deal of that terror which unmanned me at first. I supposed it was despair that strung my nerves.

'It may look like boasting – but what I tell you is truth – I began to reflect how magnificent a thing it was to die in such a manner, and how foolish it was in me to think of so paltry a consideration as my own individual life, in view of so wonderful a manifestation of God's power. I do believe that I blushed with shame when this idea crossed my mind. After a little while I became possessed with the keenest curiosity about the whirl itself. I positively felt a *wish* to explore its depths, even at the sacrifice I was going to make; and my principal grief was that I should never be able to tell my old companions on shore about the mysteries I should see. These, no doubt, were singular fancies to occupy a man's mind in such extremity – and I have often thought since, that the revolutions of the boat around the pool might have rendered me a little light-headed.

'There was another circumstance which tended to restore my self-possession; and this was the cessation of the wind, which could not reach us in our present situation – for, as you saw for yourself, the belt of the surf is considerably lower than the general bed of the ocean, and this latter now towered above us, a high, black, mountainous ridge. If you have never been at sea in a heavy gale, you can form no idea of the confusion of mind occasioned by the wind and spray together. They blind, deafen, and strangle you, and take away all power of action or reflection. But we were now, in a great measure, rid of these annoyances – just as death-condemned felons in prison are allowed petty indulgences, forbidden them while their doom is yet uncertain.

'How often we made the circuit of the belt it is impossible to say. We careered round and round for perhaps an hour, flying rather than floating, getting gradually more and more into the middle of the surge, and then nearer and nearer to its horrible inner edge. All this time I had never let go of the ring-bolt. My brother was at the stern, holding on to a small empty water-cask which had been securely lashed under the coop of the counter, and was the only thing on deck that had not been swept overboard when the gale first took us. As we approached the brink of the pit he let go his hold upon this, and made for the ring, from which, in the agony of his terror, he endeavored to force my hands, as it was not large enough to afford us both a secure grasp. I never felt deeper grief than when I saw him attempt this act – although I knew he was a madman when he did it – a raving maniac through sheer fright. I did not care, however, to contest the point with him. I knew it could make no difference whether either of us held on at all; so I let him have the bolt, and went astern to the cask. This there was no great difficulty in doing; for the smack flew round steadily enough, and upon an even keel – only swaying to and fro with the immense sweeps and swelters of the whirl. Scarcely had I secured myself in my new position, when we gave a wild lurch to starboard, and rushed headlong into the abyss. I muttered a hurried prayer to God, and thought all was over.

'As I felt the sickening sweep of the descent, I had instinctively tightened my hold upon the barrel, and closed my eyes. For some seconds I dared not open them – while I expected instant destruction, and wondered that I was not already in my death-struggles with the water. But moment after moment elapsed. I still lived. The sense of falling had ceased; and the motion of the vessel seemed much as it had been before, while in the

belt of foam, with the exception that she now lay
more along. I took courage and looked once again
upon the scene.

'Never shall I forget the sensation of awe,
horror, and admiration with which I gazed about
me. The boat appeared to be hanging, as if by
magic, midway down, upon the interior surface
of a funnel vast in circumference, prodigious in
depth, and whose perfectly smooth sides might
have been mistaken for ebony, but for the bewildering rapidity with which they spun around, and for
the gleaming and ghastly radiance they shot forth,
as the rays of the full moon, from that circular rift
amid the clouds which I have already described,
streamed in a flood of golden glory along the
black walls, and far down into the inmost recesses
of the abyss.

'At first I was too much confused to observe
anything accurately. The general burst of terrific
grandeur was all that I beheld. When I recovered
myself a little, however, my gaze fell instinctively
downward. In this direction I was able to obtain
an unobstructed view, from the manner in which
the smack hung on the inclined surface of the pool.
She was quite upon an even keel – that is to say,
her deck lay in a plane parallel with that of the
water – but this latter sloped at an angle of more
than forty-five degrees, so that we seemed to be
lying upon our beam-ends. I could not help observing, nevertheless, that I had scarcely more difficulty in maintaining my hold and footing in this

situation, than if we had been upon a dead level; and this, I suppose, was owing to the speed at which we revolved.

'The rays of the moon seemed to search the very bottom of the profound gulf; but still I could make out nothing distinctly on account of a thick mist in which everything there was enveloped, and over which there hung a magnificent rainbow, like that narrow and tottering bridge which Mussulmen say is the only pathway between Time and Eternity. This mist, or spray, was no doubt occasioned by the clashing of the great walls of the funnel, as they all met together at the bottom – but the yell that went up to the Heavens from out of that mist I dare not attempt to describe.

'Our first slide into the abyss itself, from the belt of foam above, had carried us to a great distance down the slope; but our farther descent was by no means proportionate. Round and round we swept – not with any uniform movement – but in dizzying swings and jerks, that sent us sometimes only a few hundred yards – sometimes nearly the complete circuit of the whirl. Our progress downward, at each revolution, was slow, but very perceptible.

'Looking about me upon the wide waste of liquid ebony on which we were thus borne, I perceived that our boat was not the only object in the embrace of the whirl. Both above and below us were visible fragments of vessels, large masses of building-timber and trunks of trees, with many smaller articles, such as pieces of house furniture, broken boxes, barrels and staves. I have already described the unnatural curiosity which had taken the place of my original terrors. It appeared to grow upon me as I drew nearer and nearer to my dreadful doom. I now began to watch, with a strange interest, the numerous things that floated in our company. I *must* have been delirious, for I even sought *amusement* in speculating upon the relative velocities of their several descents toward the foam below. "This fir-tree," I found myself at one time saying, "will certainly be the next thing that takes the awful plunge and disappears," – and then I was disappointed to find that the wreck of a Dutch merchant ship overtook it and went down before. At length, after making several guesses of this nature, and being deceived in all – this fact – the fact of my invariable miscalculation, set me upon a train of reflection that made my limbs again tremble, and my heart beat heavily once more.

'It was not a new terror that thus affected me, but the dawn of a more exciting *hope*. This hope arose partly from memory, and partly from present observation. I called to mind the great variety of buoyant matter that strewed the coast of Lofoden, having been absorbed and then thrown forth by the Moskoe-ström. By far the greater number of the articles were shattered in the most extraordinary way – so chafed and roughened as to have the appearance of being stuck full of splinters – but then I distinctly recollected that there were *some* of them which were not disfigured at all. Now I could not account for this difference except by supposing that the roughened fragments were the only ones which had been *completely absorbed* – that the others had entered the whirl at so late a period of the tide, or, from some reason, had descended so slowly after entering, that they did not reach the bottom before the turn of the flood came, or of the ebb, as the case may be. I conceived it possible, in either instance, that they might thus be whirled up again to the level of the ocean, without undergoing the fate of those which had been drawn in more early or absorbed more rapidly. I made, also, three important observations. The first was, that as a general rule, the larger the bodies were, the more rapid their descent – the second, that, between two masses of equal extent, the one spherical, and the other *of any other shape*, the superiority in speed of descent was with the sphere – the third, that, between two masses of equal size, the one cylindrical, and the other of any other shape, the cylinder was absorbed the more slowly. Since my escape, I have had several conversations on this subject with an old schoolmaster of the district; and it was from him that I learned the use of the words "cylinder" and "sphere". He explained to me – although I have forgotten the explanation – how what I observed was, in fact, the natural consequence of the forms of the floating fragments – and showed me how it happened that a cylinder, swimming in a vortex, offered more resistance to its suction, and was drawn in with greater difficulty than an equally bulky body, of any form whatever.*

'There was one startling circumstance which went a great way in enforcing these observations, and rendering me anxious to turn them to account, and this was that, at every revolution, we passed something like a barrel, or else the yard or the mast of a vessel, while many of these things which had been on our level when I first opened my eyes upon the wonders of the whirlpool, were now high up above us, and seemed to have moved but little from their original station.

'I no longer hesitated what to do. I resolved to lash myself securely to the water-cask upon which I now held, to cut it loose from the counter, and to throw myself with it into the water. I attracted my brother's attention by signs, pointed to the floating barrels that came near us, and did every-thing in my power to make him understand what I was about to do. I thought at length that he comprehended my design – but, whether this was the case or not, he shook his head despairingly, and refused to move from his station by the ring-bolt. It was impossible to reach him; the emer-gency admitted to no delay; and so, with a bitter struggle, I resigned him to his fate, fastened

* See Archimedes, *De Incidentibus in Fluido* – lib. 2.

myself to the cask by means of the lashings which secured it to the counter, and precipitated myself with it into the sea, without another moment's hesitation.

'The result was precisely what I had hoped it might be. As it is myself who now tell you this tale – as you see that I *did* escape – and as you are already in possession of the mode in which this escape was effected, and must therefore anticipate all that I have farther to say – I will bring my story quickly to conclusion. It might have been an hour, or thereabout, after my quitting the smack, when, having descended to a vast distance beneath me, it made three or four wild gyrations in rapid succession, and, bearing my loved brother with it, plunged headlong, at once and for ever, into the chaos of foam below. The barrel to which I was attached sunk very little farther than half the distance between the bottom of the gulf and the spot at which I leaped overboard, before a great change took place in the character of the whirl-pool. The slope of the sides of the vast funnel became momently less and less steep. The gyrations of the whirl grew, gradually, less and less violent. By degrees, the froth and the rainbow disappeared, and the bottom of the gulf seemed slowly to uprise. The sky was clear, the winds had gone down, and the full moon was setting radiantly in the west, when I found myself on the surface of the ocean, in full view of the shores of Lofoden, and above the spot where the pool of the

Moskoe-ström *had been*. It was the hour of the slack – but the sea still heaved in mountainous waves from the effects of the hurricane. I was borne violently into the channel of the Ström, and in a few minutes, was hurried down the coast into the "grounds" of the fishermen. A boat picked me up – exhausted from fatigue – and (now that the danger was removed) speechless from the memory of its horror. Those who drew me on board were my old mates and daily companions – but they knew me no more than they would have known a traveller from the spirit-land. My hair, which had been raven black the day before, was as white as you see it now. They say too that the whole expression of my countenance had changed. I told them my story – they did not believe it. I now tell it to *you* – and I can scarcely expect you to put more faith in it than did the merry fishermen of Lofoden.'

True! – nervous – very, very dreadfully nervous I had been and am; but why *will* you say that I am mad? The disease had sharpened my senses – not destroyed – not dulled them. Above all was the sense of hearing acute. I heard all things in the heaven and in the earth. I heard many things in hell. How, then, am I mad? Hearken! and observe how healthily – how calmly I can tell you the whole story.

It is impossible to say how first the idea entered my brain; but once conceived, it haunted me day and night. Object there was none. Passion there was none. I loved the old man. He had never wronged me. He had never given me insult. For his gold I had no desire. I think it was his eye! yes, it was this! One of his eyes resembled that of a vulture – a pale blue eye, with a film over it. Whenever it fell upon me, my blood ran cold; and so by degrees – very gradually – I made up my mind to take the life of the old man, and thus rid myself of the eye for ever.

Now this is the point. You fancy me mad. Madmen know nothing. But you should have seen

me. You should have seen how wisely I proceeded
– with what caution – with what foresight – with
what dissimulation I went to work! I was never
kinder to the old man than during the whole week
before I killed him. And every night, about midnight, I turned the latch of his door and opened it
– oh, so gently! And then, when I had made an
opening sufficient for my head, I put in a dark
lantern, all closed, closed, so that no light shone
out, and then I thrust in my head. Oh, you would
have laughed to see how cunningly I thrust it in! I
moved it slowly – very, very slowly, so that I
might not disturb the old man's sleep. It took me
an hour to place my whole head within the opening so far that I could see him as he lay upon his
bed. Ha! – would a madman have been so wise as
this? And then, when my head was well in the
room, I undid the lantern cautiously – oh, so
cautiously – cautiously (for the hinges creaked) – I
undid it just so much that a single thin ray fell upon
the vulture eye. And this I did for seven long nights –
every night just at midnight – but I found the eye
always closed; and so it was impossible to do the
work; for it was not the old man who vexed me, but
his Evil Eye. And every morning, when the day
broke, I went boldly into the chamber, and spoke
courageously to him, calling him by name in a
hearty tone, and inquiring how he had passed the
night. So you see he would have been a very profound old man, indeed, to suspect that every night,
just at twelve, I looked in upon him while he slept.

Upon the eighth night I was more than usually cautious in opening the door. A watch's minute hand moves more quickly than did mine. Never before that night had I *felt* the extent of my own powers – of my sagacity. I could scarcely contain my feelings of triumph. To think that there I was, opening the door, little by little, and he not even to dream of my secret deeds or thoughts. I fairly chuckled at the idea; and perhaps he heard me; for he moved on the bed suddenly, as if startled. Now you may think that I drew back – but no. His room was as black as pitch with the thick darkness (for the shutters were close fastened, through fear of robbers), and so I knew that he could not see the opening of the door, and I kept pushing it on steadily, steadily.

I had my head in, and was about to open the lantern, when my thumb slipped upon the tin fastening, and the old man sprang up in the bed, crying out – 'Who's there?'

I kept quite still and said nothing. For a whole hour I did not move a muscle, and in the mean time I did not hear him lie down. He was still sitting up in the bed listening; just as I have done, night after night, hearkening to the death watches in the wall.

Presently I heard a slight groan, and I knew it was the groan of mortal terror. It was not a groan of pain or of grief – oh, no! – it was the low stifled sound that arises from the bottom of the soul when overcharged with awe. I knew the sound well. Many a night, just at midnight, when all the world slept, it has welled up from my own bosom, deepening, with its dreadful echo, the terrors that distracted me. I say I knew it well. I knew what the old man felt, and pitied him, although I chuckled at heart. I knew that he had been lying awake ever since the first slight noise, when he had turned in the bed. His fears had been ever since growing upon him. He had been trying to fancy them causeless, but could not. He had been saying to himself – 'It is nothing but the wind in the chimney – it is only a mouse crossing the floor,' or 'it is merely a cricket which has made a single chirp.' Yes, he had been trying to comfort himself with these suppositions but he had found all in vain. *All in vain*; because Death, in approaching him, had stalked with his black shadow before him, and enveloped the victim. And it was the mournful influence of the unperceived shadow that caused him to feel – although he neither saw nor heard – to *feel* the presence of my head within the room.

When I had waited a long time, very patiently, without hearing him lie down, I resolved to open a little – a very, very little crevice in the lantern. So I opened it – you cannot imagine how stealthily, stealthily – until, at length, a single dim ray, like the thread of the spider, shot from out the crevice and full upon the vulture eye.

It was open – wide, wide open – and I grew furious as I gazed upon it. I saw it with perfect distinctness – all a dull blue, with a hideous veil over it that chilled the very marrow in my bones; but I could see nothing else of the old man's face or person: for I had directed the ray as if by instinct, precisely upon the damned spot.

And now have I not told you that what you mistake for madness is but over-acuteness of the senses? – now, I say, there came to my ears a low, dull, quick sound, such as a watch makes when enveloped in cotton. I knew *that* sound well too. It was the beating of the old man's heart. It increased my fury, as the beating of a drum stimulates the soldier into courage.

But even yet I refrained and kept still. I scarcely breathed. I held the lantern motionless. I tried how steadily I could maintain the ray upon the eye. Meantime the hellish tattoo of the heart increased. It grew quicker and quicker, and louder and louder every instant. The old man's terror *must* have been extreme! It grew louder, I say, louder every moment! – do you mark me well? I have told you that I am nervous: so I am. And now at the dead hour of the night, amid the dreadful silence of that old house, so strange a noise as this excited me to uncontrollable terror. Yet, for some minutes longer I refrained and stood still. But the beating grew louder, louder! I thought the heart must burst. And now a new anxiety seized me – the sound would be heard by a neighbor! The old man's hour had come! With a loud yell, I threw open the lantern and leaped into the room. He shrieked once – once only. In an instant I dragged him to the floor, and pulled the heavy bed over him. I then smiled gaily, to find the deed so far done. But, for many minutes, the heart beat on with a muffled sound. This, however, did not vex me, it would not be heard through the wall. At length it ceased. The old man was dead. I removed the bed and examined the corpse. Yes, he was stone, stone dead. I placed my hand upon the heart and held it there many minutes. There was no pulsation. He was stone dead. His eye would trouble me no more.

If still you think me mad, you will think so no longer when I describe the wise precautions I took for the concealment of the body. The night waned, and I worked hastily, but in silence. First of all I dismembered the corpse. I cut off the head and the arms and the legs.

I then took up three planks from the flooring of the chamber, and deposited all between the scantlings. I then replaced the boards so cleverly, so cunningly, that no human eye – not even *his* – could have detected anything wrong. There was nothing to wash out – no stain of any kind – no blood-spot whatever. I had been too wary for that. A tub had caught all – ha! ha!

When I had made an end of these labors, it was four o'clock – still dark as midnight. As the bell sounded the hour, there came a knocking at the street door. I went down to open it with a light heart – for what had I *now* to fear? There entered three men, who introduced themselves, with perfect suavity, as officers of the police. A shriek had been heard by a neighbor during the night; suspicion of foul play had been aroused; information had been lodged at the police office, and they (the officers) had been deputed to search the premises.

I smiled – for *what* had I to fear? I bade the gentlemen welcome. The shriek, I said, was my own in a dream. The old man, I mentioned, was absent in the country. I took my visitors all over the house. I bade them search – search *well*. I led them, at length, to *his* chamber. I showed them his treasures secure, undisturbed. In the enthusiasm of my confidence, I brought chairs into the room, and desired them *here* to rest from their fatigues, while I myself, in the wild audacity of my perfect triumph, placed my own seat upon the very spot beneath which reposed the corpse of the victim.

The officers were satisfied. My *manner* had convinced them. I was singularly at ease. They sat, and while I answered cheerily, they chatted of familiar things. But, ere long, I felt myself getting pale and wished them gone. My head ached, and I fancied a ringing in my ears: but still they sat and still chatted. The ringing became more distinct: it continued and became more distinct: I talked more freely to get rid of the feeling: but it continued and gained definitiveness – until, at length, I found that the noise was *not* within my ears.

No doubt I now grew *very* pale; but I talked

more fluently, and with a heightened voice. Yet the sound increased – and what could I do? It was *a low, dull, quick sound – much such a sound as a watch makes when enveloped in cotton.* I gasped for breath – and yet the officers heard it not. I talked more quickly – and vehemently; but the noise steadily increased. I arose and argued about trifles, in a high key and with violent gesticulations, but the noise steadily increased. Why *would* they not be gone? I paced the floor to and fro with heavy strides, as if excited to fury by the observation of the men – but the noise steadily increased. Oh God! what *could* I do? I foamed – I raved – I swore! I swung the chair upon which I had been sitting, and grated it upon the boards, but the noise arose over all and continually increased. It grew louder – louder – *louder!* And still the men chatted pleasantly, and smiled. Was it possible they heard not? Almighty God! – no, no! They heard! – they suspected! – they *knew!* – they were making a mockery of my horror! – this I thought, and this I think. But anything was better than this agony! Anything was more tolerable than this derision! I could bear those hypocritical smiles no longer! I felt that I must scream or die! – and now – again! – hark! louder! louder! louder! *louder!* –

'Villains!' I shrieked, 'dissemble no more! I admit the deed! – tear up the planks! – here, here! – it is the beating of his hideous heart!'

The Oblong Box

Some years ago, I engaged passage from Charleston, SC, to the city of New York, in the fine packet-ship *Independence*, Captain Hardy. We were to sail on the fifteenth of the month (June), weather permitting; and, on the fourteenth, I went on board to arrange some matters in my state-room.

I found that we were to have a great many passengers, including a more than usual number of ladies. On the list were several of my acquaintances; and among other names, I was rejoiced to see that of Mr Cornelius Wyatt, a young artist, for whom I entertained feelings of warm friendship. He had been with me a fellow-student at C— University, where we were very much together. He had the ordinary temperament of genius, and was a compound of misanthropy, sensibility, and enthusiasm. To these qualities he united the warmest and truest heart which ever beat in a human bosom.

I observed that his name was carded upon *three* state-rooms: and, upon again referring to the list of passengers, I found that he had engaged passage

for himself, wife, and two sisters – his own. The
state-rooms were sufficiently roomy, and each had
two berths, one above the other. These berths, to
be sure, were so exceedingly narrow as to be
insufficient for more than one person; still, I could
not comprehend why there were *three* state-rooms
for these four persons. I was, just at that epoch, in
one of those moody frames of mind which make a
man abnormally inquisitive about trifles: and I
confess, with shame, that I busied myself in a
variety of ill-bred and preposterous conjectures
about this matter of the super-numerary state-
room. It was no business of mine, to be sure, but
with none the less pertinacity did I occupy myself
in attempts to resolve the enigma. At last I reached
a conclusion which wrought in me great wonder
why I had not arrived at it before. 'It is a scrvant,
of course,' I said; 'what a fool I am, not sooner to
have thought of so obvious a solution!' And then I
again repaired to the list – but here I saw distinctly
that *no* servant was to come with the party: although, in fact, it had been the original design to
bring one – for the words 'and servant' had been
first written and then overscored. 'Oh, extra baggage, to be sure,' I now said to myself – 'something
he wishes not to be put in the hold – something to
be kept under his own eye – ah, I have it – a
painting or so – and this is what he has been
bargaining about with Nicolino, the Italian Jew.'
This idea satisfied mc, and I dismissed my curiosity for the nonce.

Wyatt's two sisters I knew very well, and most amiable and clever girls they were. His wife he had newly married, and I had never yet seen her. He had often talked about her in my presence, however, and in his usual style of enthusiasm. He described her as of surpassing beauty, wit and accomplishment. I was, therefore, quite anxious to make her acquaintance.

On the day in which I visited the ship (the fourteenth), Wyatt and party were also to visit it – so the captain informed me – and I waited on board an hour longer than I had designed, in hope of being presented to the bride; but then an apology came. 'Mrs W. was a little indisposed, and would decline coming on board until tomorrow, at the hour of sailing.'

The morrow having arrived, I was going from my hotel to the wharf, when Captain Hardy met me and said that, 'owing to circumstances' (a stupid but convenient phrase), 'he rather thought the *Independence* would not sail for a day or two, and that when all was ready, he would send up and let me know.' This I thought strange, for there was a stiff southerly breeze; but as 'the circumstances' were not forthcoming, although I pumped for them with much perseverance, I had nothing to do but to return home and digest my impatience at leisure.

I did not receive the expected message from the captain for nearly a week. It came at length, however, and I immediately went on board. The ship was crowded with passengers, and everything was in the bustle attendant upon making sail. Wyatt's party arrived in about ten minutes after myself. There were the two sisters, the bride, and the artist – the latter in one of his customary fits of moody misanthropy. I was too well used to these, however, to pay them any special attention. He did not even introduce me to his wife: this courtesy devolving, perforce, upon his sister Marian – a very sweet and intelligent girl, who, in a few hurried words, made us acquainted.

Mrs Wyatt had been closely veiled; and when she raised her veil, in acknowledging my bow, I confess that I was very profoundly astonished. I should have been much more so, however, had not long experience advised me not to trust, with too implicit a reliance, the enthusiastic description of my friend, the artist, when indulging in comments upon the loveliness of woman. When beauty was the theme, I well knew with what facility he soared into the regions of the purely ideal.

The truth is, I could not help regarding Mrs Wyatt as a decidedly plain-looking woman. If not positively ugly, she was not, I think, very far from it. She was dressed, however, in exquisite taste – and then I had no doubt that she had captivated my friend's heart by the more enduring graces of the intellect and soul. She said very few words, and passed at once into her state-room with Mr W.

My old inquisitiveness now returned. There was *no* servant – *that* was a settled point. I looked, therefore, for the extra baggage. After some delay, a cart arrived at the wharf, with an oblong pine box, which was everything that seemed to be expected. Immediately upon its arrival we made sail, and in a short time were safely over the bar and standing out to sea.

The box in question was, as I say, oblong. It was about six feet in length by two and a half in breadth; I observed it attentively, and like to be precise. Now this shape was *peculiar*; and no sooner had I seen it, than I took credit to myself for the accuracy of my guessing. I had reached the conclusion, it will be remembered, that the extra baggage of my friend, the artist, would prove to be pictures, or at least a picture; for I knew he had been for several weeks in conference with Nicolino: and now here was a box, which, from its shape, *could* possibly contain nothing in the world but a copy of Leonardo's 'Last Supper'; and a copy of this very 'Last Supper', done by Rubini the younger, at Florence, I had known, for some time, to be in the possession of Nicolino. This point, therefore, I considered as sufficiently settled. I chuckled excessively when I thought of my acumen. It was the first time I had ever known Wyatt to keep from me any of his artistical secrets; but here he evidently intended to steal a march upon me, and smuggle a fine picture to New York, under my very nose, expecting me to know nothing of the matter. I resolved to quiz him *well*, now and hereafter.

One thing, however, annoyed me not a little. The box did not go into the extra state-room. It was deposited in Wyatt's own; and there, too, it remained, occupying very nearly the whole of the floor – no doubt to the exceeding discomfort of the artist and his wife; this the more especially as the tar or paint with which it was lettered in sprawling capitals, emitted a strong, disagreeable, and, to *my* fancy, a peculiarly disgusting odor. On the lid were painted the words – '*Mrs Adelaide Curtis, Albany, New York. Charge of Cornelius Wyatt, Esq. This side up. To be handled with care.*'

Now, I was aware that Mrs Adelaide Curtis, of Albany, was the artist's wife's mother; but then I looked upon the whole address as a mystification, intended especially for myself. I made up my mind, of course, that the box and contents would never get farther north than the studio of my misanthropic friend, in Chambers Street, New York.

For the first three or four days we had fine weather, although the wind was dead ahead, having chopped round to the northward, immediately upon our losing sight of the coast. The passengers were, consequently, in high spirits and disposed to be social. I *must* except, however, Wyatt and his sisters, who behaved stiffly, and, I could not help thinking, uncourteously to the rest of the party. *Wyatt's* conduct I did not so much regard. He was gloomy, even beyond his usual habit – in fact he was *morose* – but in him I was prepared for eccentricity. For the sisters, however, I could make no excuse. They secluded themselves in their state-rooms during the greater part of the passage, and absolutely refused, although I repeatedly urged them, to hold communication with any person on board.

Mrs Wyatt herself was far more agreeable. That is to say, she was *chatty*; and to be chatty is no slight recommendation at sea. She became *excessively* intimate with most of the ladies; and, to my profound astonishment, evinced no equivocal disposition to coquet with the men. She amused us all very much. I say '*amused*' – and scarcely know how to explain myself. The truth is, I soon found that Mrs W. was far oftener laughed *at* than *with*. The gentlemen said little about her; but the ladies, in a little while, pronounced her 'a good-hearted thing, rather indifferent-looking, totally uneducated, and decidedly vulgar'. The great wonder was, how Wyatt had been entrapped into such a match. Wealth was the general solution – but this I knew to be no solution at all; for Wyatt had told me that she neither brought him a dollar nor had any expectations from any source whatever. 'He had married,' he said, 'for love, and for love only; and his bride was far more than worthy of his love.' When I thought of these expressions, on the part of my friend, I confess that I felt indescribably puzzled. Could it be possible that he was taking leave of his senses? What else could I think? *He*, so refined, so intellectual, so fastidious, with so exquisite a perception of the faulty, and so keen an appreciation of the beautiful! To be sure, the lady seemed especially fond of *him* – particularly so in his absence – when she made herself ridiculous by frequent quotations of what had been said by her 'beloved husband, Mr Wyatt'. The word 'husband' seemed forever – to use one of her own delicate expressions – forever 'on the tip of her tongue'. In the mean time, it was observed by all on board, that he avoided *her* in the most pointed manner, and, for the most part, shut himself up alone in his state-room where, in fact, he might have been said to live altogether, leaving his wife at full liberty to amuse herself as she thought best, in the public society of the main cabin.

My conclusion, from what I saw and heard, was, that the artist, by some unaccountable freak of fate, or perhaps in some fit of enthusiastic and fanciful passion, had been induced to unite himself with a person altogether beneath him, and that the natural result, entire and speedy disgust had ensued. I pitied him from the bottom of my heart – but could not, for that reason, quite forgive his incommunicativeness in the matter of the 'Last Supper'. For this I resolved to have my revenge.

One day he came upon deck, and, taking his arm as had been my wont, I sauntered with him backward and forward. His gloom, however (which I considered quite natural under the circumstances), seemed entirely unabated. He said little, and that moodily, and with evident effort. I ventured a jest or two, and he made a sickening attempt at a smile. Poor fellow! – as I thought of *his wife*, I wondered that he could have heart to put on even the semblance of mirth. At last I ventured a home thrust. I determined to commence a series of covert insinuations, or innuendoes, about the oblong box – just to let him perceive, gradually, that I was *not* altogether the butt, or victim, of his little bit of pleasant mystification. My first observation was by way of opening a masked battery. I said something about the 'peculiar shape of *that* box'; and, as I spoke the words, I smiled knowingly, winked, and touched him gently with my forefinger in the ribs.

The manner in which Wyatt received this harmless pleasantry convinced me, at once, that he was mad. At first he stared at me as if he found it impossible to comprehend the witticism of my remark; but as its point seemed slowly to make its way into his brain, his eyes, in the same proportion, seemed protruding from their sockets. Then he grew very red – then hideously pale – then, as if highly amused with what I had insinuated, he began a loud and boisterous laugh, which, to my astonishment, he kept up, with gradually increasing vigor, for ten minutes or more. In conclusion, he fell flat and heavily upon the deck. When I ran to uplift him, to all appearance he was *dead*.

I called assistance, and, with much difficulty, we brought him to himself. Upon reviving he spoke incoherently for some time. At length we bled him and put him to bed. The next morning he was quite recovered, so far as regarded his mere bodily health. Of his mind I say nothing, of course. I avoided him during the rest of the passage, by advice of the captain, who seemed to coincide with me altogether in my views of his insanity, but cautioned me to say nothing on this head to any person on board.

Several circumstances occurred immediately after this fit of Wyatt's, which contributed to heighten the curiosity with which I was already possessed. Among other things, this: I had been nervous – drank too much strong green tea, and slept ill at night – in fact, for two nights I could not be properly said to sleep at all. Now, my state-room opened into the main cabin, or dining-room, as did those of all the single men on board. Wyatt's three rooms were in the after-cabin, which was separated from the main one by a slight sliding door, never locked even at night. As we were almost constantly on a wind, and the breeze was not a little stiff, the ship heeled to leeward very considerably; and whenever her starboard side was to leeward, the sliding door between the cabins slid open, and so remained, nobody taking the trouble to get up and shut it. But my berth was in such a position, that when my own state-room door was open, as well as the sliding door in question (and my own door was *always* open on account of the heat) I could see into the after-cabin quite distinctly, and just at that portion of it, too, where were situated the state-rooms of Mr Wyatt. Well, during two nights (*not* consecutive) while I lay awake, I clearly saw Mrs W., about eleven o'clock upon each night, steal cautiously from the state-room of Mr W., and enter the extra room, where she remained until daybreak, when she was called by her husband and went back. That they were virtually separated was clear. They had separate apartments – no doubt in contemplation of a more permanent divorce; and here, after all, I thought was the mystery of the extra state-room.

There was another circumstance, too, which interested me much. During the two wakeful nights in question, and immediately after the disappearance of Mrs Wyatt into the extra state-room, I was attracted by certain singular, cautious, subdued noises in that of her husband. After listening to them for some time, with thoughtful attention, I at length succeeded perfectly in translating their import. They were sounds occasioned by the artist in prying open the oblong box, by means of a chisel and mallet – the latter being apparently muffled, or deadened, by some soft woollen or cotton substance in which its head was enveloped.

In this manner I fancied I could distinguish the precise moment when he fairly disengaged the lid – also, that I could determine when he removed it altogether, and when he deposited it upon the lower berth in his room; this latter point I knew, for example, by certain slight taps which the lid made in striking against the wooden edges of the berth, as he endeavored to lay it down *very* gently – there being no room for it on the floor. After this there was a dead stillness, and I heard nothing more, upon either occasion, until nearly daybreak; unless, perhaps, I may mention a low sobbing, or murmuring sound, so very much suppressed as to be nearly inaudible – if, indeed, the whole of this latter noise were not rather produced by my own imagination. I say it seemed to *resemble* sobbing or sighing – but, of course, it could not have been either. I rather think it was a ringing in my own ears. Mr Wyatt, no doubt, according to custom, was merely giving the rein to one of his hobbies – indulging in one of his fits of artistic enthusiasm. He had opened his oblong box, in order to feast his eyes on the pictorial treasure within. There was nothing in this, however, to make him *sob*. I repeat, therefore, that it must have been simply a freak of my own fancy, distempered by good Captain Hardy's green tea. Just before dawn, on each of the two nights of which I speak, I distinctly heard Mr Wyatt replace the lid upon the oblong box, and force the nails into their old places by means of the muffled mallet. Having done this, he issued from his state-room, fully dressed, and proceeded to call Mrs W. from hers.

We had been at sea seven days, and were now

off Cape Hatteras, when there came a tremendously heavy blow from the southwest. We were, in a measure, prepared for it, however, as the weather had been holding out threats for some time. Everything was made snug, alow and aloft; and as the wind steadily freshened, we lay to, at length, under spanker and foretopsail, both double-reefed.

In this trim we rode safely enough for forty-eight hours – the ship proving herself an excellent sea-boat in many respects, and shipping no water of any consequence. At the end of this period, however, the gale had freshened into a hurricane, and our after-sail split into ribbons, bringing us so much in the trough of the water that we shipped several prodigious seas, one immediately after the other. By this accident we lost three men overboard with the caboose, and nearly the whole of the larboard bulwarks. Scarcely had we recovered our senses, before the foretopsail went into shreds, when we got up a storm stay-sail, and with this did pretty well for some hours, the ship heading the sea much more steadily than before.

The gale still held on, however, and we saw no signs of its abating. The rigging was found to be ill-fitted, and greatly strained; and on the third day of the blow, about five in the afternoon, our mizzen-mast, in a heavy lurch to windward, went by the board. For an hour or more, we tried in vain to get rid of it, on account of the prodigious rolling of the ship; and, before we had succeeded, the carpenter came aft and announced four feet water in the hold. To add to our dilemma, we found the pumps choked and nearly useless.

All was now confusion and despair – but an effort was made to lighten the ship by throwing overboard as much of her cargo as could be reached, and by cutting away the two masts that remained. This we at last accomplished – but we were still unable to do anything at the pumps: and, in the mean time, the leak gained on us very fast.

At sundown, the gale had sensibly diminished in violence, and, as the sea went down with it, we still entertained faint hopes of saving ourselves in the boats. At eight p.m., the clouds broke away to windward, and we had the advantage of a full moon – a piece of good fortune which served wonderfully to cheer our drooping spirits.

After incredible labor we succeeded, at length, in getting the long-boat over the side without material accident, and into this we crowded the whole of the crew and most of the passengers. This party made off immediately, and, after undergoing much suffering, finally arrived, in safety, at Ocracoke Inlet, on the third day after the wreck.

Fourteen passengers, with the captain, remained on board, resolving to trust their fortunes to the jolly-boat at the stern. We lowered it without difficulty, although it was only by a miracle that we prevented it from swamping as it touched the water. It contained, when afloat, the captain and his wife, Mr Wyatt and party, a Mexican officer, wife, four children, and myself, with a negro valet.

We had no room, of course, for anything except a few positively necessary instruments, some provisions, and the clothes upon our backs. No one had thought of even attempting to save anything more. What must have been the astonishment of all, then, when, having proceeded a few fathoms from the ship, Mr Wyatt stood up in the stern-sheets, and coolly demanded of Captain Hardy that the boat should be put back for the purpose of taking in his oblong box!

'Sit down, Mr Wyatt,' replied the captain, somewhat sternly, 'you will capsize us if you do not sit quite still. Our gunwale is almost in the water now.'

'The box!' vociferated Mr Wyatt, still standing – 'the box, I say! Captain Hardy, you cannot, you *will* not refuse me. Its weight will be but a trifle – it is nothing – mere nothing. By the mother who bore you – for the love of Heaven – by your hope of salvation, I *implore* you to put back for the box!'

The captain, for a moment, seemed touched by the earnest appeal of the artist, but he regained his stern composure, and merely said:

'Mr Wyatt, you are *mad*. I cannot listen to you. Sit down, I say, or you will swamp the boat. Stay – hold him – seize him! – he is about to spring overboard! There – I knew it – he is over!'

As the captain said this, Mr Wyatt, in fact, sprang from the boat, and, as we were yet in the lee of the wreck, succeeded, by almost superhuman exertion, in getting hold of a rope which hung from the fore-chains. In another moment he was on board, and rushing frantically down into the cabin.

In the mean time, we had been swept astern of the ship, and being quite out of her lee, were at the mercy of the tremendous sea which was still running. We made a determined effort to put back, but our little boat was like a feather in the breath of the tempest. We saw at a glance that the doom of the unfortunate artist was sealed.

As our distance from the wreck rapidly increased, the madman (for as such only could we regard him) was seen to emerge from the companionway, up which by dint of strength that appeared gigantic, he dragged, bodily, the oblong box. While we gazed in the extremity of astonishment, he passed, rapidly, several turns of a three-inch rope, first around the box and then around his body. In another instant both body and box were in the sea – disappearing suddenly, at once and for ever.

We lingered awhile sadly upon our oars, with our eyes riveted upon the spot. At length, we pulled away. The silence remained unbroken for an hour. Finally, I hazarded a remark.

'Did you observe, captain, how suddenly they sank? Was not that an exceedingly singular thing?

I confess that I entertained some feeble hope of his final deliverance, when I saw him lash himself to the box, and commit himself to the sea.'

'They sank as a matter of course,' replied the captain, 'and that like a shot. They will soon rise again, however – *but not till the salt melts.*'

'The salt!' I ejaculated.

'Hush!' said the captain, pointing to the wife and sisters of the deceased. 'We must talk of these things at some more appropriate time.'

We suffered much, and made a narrow escape; but fortune befriended *us*, as well as our mates in the long-boat. We landed, in fine, more dead than alive, after four days of intense distress, upon the beach opposite Roanoke Island. We remained here a week, were not ill-treated by the wreckers, and at length obtained a passage to New York

About a month after the loss of the *Independence*, I happened to meet Captain Hardy in Broadway. Our conversation turned, naturally, upon the disaster, and especially upon the sad fate of poor Wyatt. I thus learned the following particulars.

The artist had engaged passage for himself, wife, two sisters and a servant. His wife was, indeed, as she had been represented, a most lovely, and most accomplished woman. On the morning of the fourteenth of June (the day in which I first visited the ship), the lady suddenly sickened and died. The young husband was frantic with grief –

but circumstances imperatively forbade the defer-
ring his voyage to New York. It was necessary to take
to her mother the corpse of his adored wife, and, on
the other hand, the universal prejudice which would
prevent his doing so openly was well known. Nine
tenths of the passengers would have abandoned the
ship rather than take passage with a dead body.

In this dilemma, Captain Hardy arranged that
the corpse, being first partially embalmed, and
packed, with a large quantity of salt, in a box of
suitable dimensions, should be conveyed on board
as merchandise. Nothing was to be said of the
lady's decease; and, as it was well understood that
Mr Wyatt had engaged passage for his wife, it
became necessary that some person should person-
ate her during the voyage. This the deceased's
lady's-maid was easily prevailed on to do. The
extra state-room, originally engaged for this girl,
during her mistress's life, was now merely retained.
In this state-room the pseudo-wife slept, of course,
every night. In the daytime she performed, to the
best of her ability, the part of her mistress – whose
person, it had been carefully ascertained, was unknown to any of the passengers on board.

My own mistake arose, naturally enough,
through too careless, too inquisitive, and too impulsive a temperament. But of late, it is a rare
thing that I sleep soundly at night. There is a
countenance which haunts me, turn as I will.
There is an hysterical laugh which will for ever
ring within my ears.

The Masque of the Red Death

The 'Red Death' had long devastated the country. No pestilence had ever been so fatal, or so hideous. Blood was its Avatar and its seal – the redness and the horror of blood. There were sharp pains, and sudden dizziness, and then profuse bleeding at the pores, with dissolution. The scarlet stains upon the body and especially upon the face of the victim, were the pest ban which shut him out from the aid and from the sympathy of his fellow-men. And the whole seizure, progress, and termination of the disease, were the incidents of half an hour.

But the Prince Prospero was happy and dauntless and sagacious. When his dominions were half depopulated, he summoned to his presence a thousand hale and light-hearted friends from among the knights and dames of his court, and with these retired to the deep seclusion of one of his castellated abbeys. This was an extensive and magnificent structure, the creation of the prince's own eccentric yet august taste. A strong and lofty wall girdled it in. This wall had gates of iron. The courtiers, having entered, brought furnaces and massy hammers and welded the bolts. They resolved to leave means neither of ingress nor egress to the sudden impulses of despair or of frenzy from within. The abbey was amply provisioned. With such precautions the courtiers might bid defiance to contagion. The external world could take care of itself. In the mean time it was folly to grieve, or to think. The prince had provided all the appliances of pleasure. There were buffoons, there were improvisatori, there were ballet-dancers, there were musicians, there was Beauty, there was wine. All these and security were within. Without was the 'Red Death'.

It was toward the close of the fifth or sixth month of his seclusion, and while the pestilence raged most furiously abroad, that the Prince Prospero entertained his thousand friends at a masked ball of the most unusual magnificence.

It was a voluptuous scene, that masquerade. But first let me tell of the rooms in which it was held. There were seven – an imperial suite. In many palaces, however, such suites form a long and straight vista, while the folding doors slide back nearly to the walls on either hand, so that the view of the whole extent is scarcely impeded. Here the case was very different; as might have been expected from the duke's love of the *bizarre*. The apartments were so irregularly disposed that the vision embraced but little more than one at a time. There was a sharp turn at every twenty or thirty yards, and at each turn a novel effect. To the right and left, in the middle of each wall, a tall and narrow Gothic window looked out upon a closed corridor which pursued the windings of the suite. These windows were of stained glass whose color varied in accordance with the prevailing hue of the decorations of the chamber into which it opened. That at the eastern extremity was hung, for example, in blue – and vividly blue were its windows. The second chamber was purple in its ornaments and tapestries, and here the panes were purple. The third was green throughout, and so were the casements. The fourth was furnished and lighted with orange – the fifth with white – the sixth with violet. The seventh apartment was closely shrouded in black velvet tapestries that hung all over the ceiling and down the walls, falling in heavy folds upon a carpet of the same material and hue. But in this chamber only, the color of the windows failed to correspond with the decorations. The panes here were scarlet – a deep blood color. Now in no one of the seven apartments was there any lamp or candelabrum, amid the profusion of golden ornaments that lay scattered to and fro or depended from the roof. There was no light of any kind emanating from lamp or candle within the suite of chambers. But in the corridors that followed the suite, there stood, opposite to each window, a heavy tripod, bearing a brazier of fire, that projected its rays through the tinted glass and so glaringly illumined the room. And thus were produced a multitude of gaudy and fantastic appearances. But in the western or black chamber the effect of the fire-light that streamed upon the dark hangings through the blood-tinted panes was ghastly in the extreme, and produced so wild a look upon the countenances of those who entered, that there were few of the company bold enough to set foot within its precincts at all.

It was in this apartment, also, that there stood against the western wall, a gigantic clock of ebony. Its pendulum swung to and fro with a dull, heavy, monotonous clang; and when the minute-hand made the circuit of the face, and the hour was to be stricken, there came from the brazen lungs of the clock a sound which was clear and loud and deep and exceedingly musical, but of so peculiar a note and emphasis that, at each lapse of an hour, the musicians of the orchestra were constrained to pause, momentarily, in their performance, to hearken to the sound; and thus the waltzers perforce ceased their evolutions; and there was a brief disconcert of the whole gay company; and, while the chimes of the clock yet rang, it was observed that the giddiest grew pale, and the more aged and sedate passed their hands over their brows as if in confused reverie or meditation. But when the echoes had fully ceased, a light laughter at once pervaded the assembly; the musicians looked at each other and smiled as if at their own nervousness and folly, and made whispering vows, each to the other, that the next chiming of the clock should produce in them no similar emotion; and then, after the lapse of sixty minutes (which embrace three thousand and six hundred seconds of the Time that flies), there came yet another chiming of the clock, and then were the same disconcert and tremulousness and meditation as before.

But, in spite of these things, it was a gay and magnificent revel. The tastes of the duke were peculiar. He had a fine eye for colors and effects. He disregarded the *decora* of mere fashion. His plans were bold and fiery, and his conceptions glowed with barbaric lustre. There are some who would have thought him mad. His followers felt that he was not. It was necessary to hear and see and touch him to be *sure* that he was not.

He had directed, in great part, the movable embellishments of the seven chambers, upon occasion of this great *fête*; and it was his own guiding taste which had given character to the masqueraders. Be sure they were grotesque. There were much glare and glitter and piquancy and phantasm – much of what has been since seen in 'Hernani'. There were arabesque figures with unsuited limbs and appointments. There were delirious fancies such as the madman fashions. There were much of the beautiful, much of the wanton, much of the *bizarre*, something of the terrible, and not a little of that which might have excited disgust. To and fro in the seven chambers there stalked, in fact, a multitude of dreams. And these – the dreams – writhed in and about, taking hue from the rooms, and causing the wild music of the orchestra to seem as the echo of their steps. And, anon, there strikes the ebony clock which stands in the hall of the velvet. And then, for a moment, all is still, and all is silent save the voice of the clock. The dreams are stiff-frozen as they stand. But the echoes of the chime die away – they have endured but an instant – and a light, half-subdued laughter floats after them as they depart. And now again the music swells, and the dreams live, and writhe to and fro more merrily than ever, taking hue from the many-tinted windows through which stream the rays from the tripods. But to the chamber which lies most westwardly of the seven there are now none of the maskers who venture; for the night is waning away; and there flows a ruddier light through the blood-colored panes; and the blackness of the sable drapery appals; and to him whose foot falls upon the sable carpet, there comes from the near clock of ebony a muffled peal more solemnly emphatic than any which reaches *their* ears who indulge in the more remote gaieties of the other apartments.

But these other apartments were densely crowded, and in them beat feverishly the heart of life. And the revel went whirlingly on, until at length there commenced the sounding of midnight upon the clock. And then the music ceased, as I have told; and the evolutions of the waltzers were quieted; and there was an uneasy cessation of all things as before. But now there were twelve strokes to be sounded by the bell of the clock; and thus it happened, perhaps, that more of thought crept, with more of time, into the meditations of the thoughtful among those who revelled. And thus too, it happened, perhaps, that before the last echoes of the last chime had utterly sunk into silence, there were many individuals in the crowd who had found leisure to become aware of the presence of a masked figure which had arrested the attention of no single individual before. And the rumor of this new presence having spread itself whisperingly around, there arose at length from the whole company a buzz, or murmur, expressive of disapprobation and surprise – then, finally, of terror, of horror, and of disgust.

In an assembly of phantasms such as I have painted it may well be supposed that no ordinary appearance could have excited such sensation. In truth the masquerade license of the night was nearly unlimited; but the figure in question had out-Heroded Herod, and gone beyond the bounds of even the prince's indefinite decorum. There are chords in the hearts of the most reckless which cannot be touched without emotion. Even with the utterly lost, to whom life and death are equally jests, there are matters of which no jest can be made. The whole company, indeed, seemed now deeply to feel that in the costume and bearing of the stranger neither wit nor propriety existed. The figure was tall and gaunt, and shrouded from head to foot in the habiliments of the grave. The mask which concealed the visage was made so nearly to resemble the countenance of a stiffened corpse that the closest scrutiny must have had difficulty in detecting the cheat. And yet all this might have been endured, if not approved, by the mad revellers around. But the mummer had gone so far as to assume the type of the Red Death. His vesture was dabbled in *blood* – and his broad brow, with all the features of the face, was be-sprinkled with the scarlet horror.

When the eyes of Prince Prospero fell upon this spectral image (which, with a slow and solemn movement, as if more fully to sustain its *rôle*, stalked to and fro among the waltzers) he was seen to be convulsed, in the first moment with a strong shudder either of terror or distaste; but, in the next, his brow reddened with rage.

'Who dares' – he demanded hoarsely of the courtiers who stood near him – 'who dares insult us with this blasphemous mockery? Seize him and unmask him – that we may know whom we have to hang, at sunrise, from the battlements!'

It was in the eastern or blue chamber in which stood the Prince Prospero as he uttered these words. They rang throughout the seven rooms loudly and clearly, for the prince was a bold and robust man, and the music had become hushed at the waving of his hand.

It was in the blue room where stood the prince, with a group of pale courtiers by his side. At first, as he spoke, there was a slight rushing movement of this group in the direction of the intruder, who, at the moment was also near at hand, and now, with deliberate and stately step, made close approach to the speaker. But from a certain nameless awe with which the mad assumptions of the mummer had inspired the whole party, there were found none who put forth hand to seize him; so that, unimpeded, he passed within a yard of the prince's person; and, while the vast assembly, as if with one impulse, shrank from the centres of the rooms to the walls, he made his way uninterruptedly, but with the same solemn and measured step which had distinguished him from the first, through the blue chamber to the purple – through the purple to the green – through the green to the orange – through this again to the white – and even thence to the violet, ere a decided movement had been made to arrest him. It was then, however, that the Prince Prospero, maddened with rage and the shame of his own momentary cowardice, rushed hurriedly through the six chambers, while none followed him on account of a deadly terror that had seized upon all. He bore aloft a drawn dagger, and had approached, in rapid impetuosity, to within three or four feet of the retreating figure, when the latter, having attained the extremity of the velvet apartment, turned suddenly and confronted his pursuer. There was a sharp cry – and the dagger dropped gleaming upon the sable carpet, upon which, instantly afterward, fell prostrate in death the Prince Prospero.

Then, summoning the wild courage of despair, a throng of the revellers at once threw themselves into the black apartment, and, seizing the mummer, whose tall figure stood erect and motionless within the shadow of the ebony clock, gasped in unutterable horror at finding the grave cerements and corpse-like mask, which they handled with so violent a rudeness, untenanted by any tangible form.

And now was acknowledged the presence of the Red Death. He had come like a thief in the night. And one by one dropped the revellers in the blood-bedewed halls of their revel, and died each in the despairing posture of his fall. And the life of the ebony clock went out with that of the last of the gay. And the flames of the tripods expired. And Darkness and Decay and the Red Death held illimitable dominion over all.

Hop-Frog

I never knew anyone so keenly alive to a joke as the king was. He seemed to live only for joking. To tell a good story of the joke kind, and to tell it well, was the surest road to his favor. Thus it happened that his seven ministers were all noted for their accomplishments as jokers. They all took after the king, too, in being large, corpulent, oily men, as well as inimitable jokers. Whether people grow fat by joking, or whether there is something in fat itself which predisposes to a joke, I have never been quite able to determine; but certain it is that a lean joker is a *rara avis in terris*.

About the refinements, or, as he called them, the 'ghosts' of wit, the king troubled himself very little. He had an especial admiration for *breadth* in a jest, and would often put up with *length*, for the sake of it. Overniceties wearied him. He would have preferred Rabelais' 'Gargantua' to the 'Zadig' of Voltaire: and, upon the whole, practical jokes suited his taste far better than verbal ones.

At the date of my narrative, professing jesters had not altogether gone out of fashion at court. Several of the great continental 'powers' still retained their 'fools', who wore motley, with caps and bells, and who were expected to be always ready with sharp witticisms, at a moment's notice, in consideration of the crumbs that fell from the royal table.

Our king, as a matter of course, retained his 'fool'. The fact is, he *required* something in the way of folly – if only to counterbalance the heavy wisdom of the seven wise men who were his ministers – not to mention himself.

His fool, or professional jester, was not *only* a fool, however. His value was trebled in the eyes of the king, by the fact of his being also a dwarf and a cripple. Dwarfs were as common at court, in those days, as fools; and many monarchs would have found it difficult to get through their days (days are rather longer at court than elsewhere) without both a jester to laugh *with*, and a dwarf to laugh *at*. But, as I have already observed, your jesters, in ninety-nine cases out of a hundred, are fat, round, and unwieldy – so that it was no small source of self-gratulation with our king that, in Hop-Frog (this was the fool's name), he possessed a triplicate treasure in one person.

I believe the name 'Hop-Frog' was *not* that given to the dwarf by his sponsors at baptism, but it was conferred upon him, by general consent of the seven ministers, on account of his inability to walk as other men do. In fact, Hop-Frog could only get along by a sort of interjectional gait – something between a leap and a wriggle – a movement that afforded illimitable amusement, and of course consolation, to the king, for (notwithstanding the protuberance of his stomach and a constitutional swelling of the head) the king, by his whole court, was accounted a capital figure.

But although Hop-Frog, through the distortion of his legs, could move only with great pain and difficulty along a road or floor, the prodigious muscular power which nature seemed to have bestowed upon his arms, by way of compensation for deficiency in the lower limbs, enabled him to perform many feats of wonderful dexterity, where trees or ropes were in question, or anything else to climb. At such exercises he certainly much more resembled a squirrel, or a small monkey, than a frog.

I am not able to say, with precision, from what country Hop-Frog originally came. It was from some barbarous region, however, that no person ever heard of – a vast distance from the court of our king. Hop-Frog, and a young girl very little less dwarfish than himself (although of exquisite proportions, and a marvellous dancer), had been forcibly carried off from their respective homes in adjoining provinces, and sent as presents to the king, by one of his ever-victorious generals.

Under these circumstances, it is not to be wondered at that a close intimacy arose between the two little captives. Indeed, they soon became sworn friends. Hop-Frog, who, although he made a great deal of sport, was by no means popular, had it not in his power to render Trippetta many services; but *she*, on account of her grace and exquisite beauty (although a dwarf), was universally admired and petted; so she possessed much influence; and never failed to use it, whenever she could, for the benefit of Hop-Frog.

On some grand state occasion – I forget what – the king determined to have a masquerade; and whenever a masquerade, or anything of that kind, occurred at our court, then the talents both of Hop-Frog and Trippetta were sure to be called into play. Hop-Frog, in especial, was so inventive in the way of getting up pageants, suggesting novel characters, and arranging costume, for masked balls, that nothing could be done, it seems, without his assistance.

The night appointed for the *fête* had arrivcd. A gorgeous hall had been fitted up, under Trippetta's eye, with every kind of device which could possibly give *éclat* to a masquerade. The whole court was in a fever of expectation. As for costumes and characters, it might well be supposed that everybody had come to a decision on such points. Many had made up their minds (as to what *rôles* they should assume) a week, or even a month, in advance; and, in fact, there was not a particle of indecision anywhere – except in the case of the king and his seven ministers. Why *they* hesitated I never could tell, unless they did it by way of a joke. More probably, they found it difficult, on account of being so fat, to make up their minds. At all events, time flew; and, as a last resort, they sent for Trippetta and Hop-Frog.

When the two little friends obeyed the summons of the king, they found him sitting at his wine with the seven members of his cabinet council; but the monarch appeared to be in a very ill humor. He knew that Hop-Frog was not fond of wine; for it excited the poor cripple almost to madness; and madness is no comfortable feeling. But the king loved his practical jokes, and took pleasure in forcing Hop-Frog to drink and (as the king called it) 'to be merry'.

'Come here, Hop-Frog,' said he, as the jester and his friend entered the room, 'swallow this bumper to the health of your absent friends [here Hop-Frog sighed] and then let us have the benefit of your invention. We want characters – *characters*, man – something novel – out of the way. We are wearied with this everlasting sameness. Come, drink! the wine will brighten your wits.'

Hop-Frog endeavored, as usual, to get up a jest in reply to these advances from the king; but the effort was too much. It happened to be the poor dwarf's birthday, and the command to drink to his 'absent friends' forced the tears to his eyes. Many large, bitter drops fell into the goblet as he took it, humbly, from the hand of the tyrant.

'Ah! ha! ha! ha!' roared the latter, as the dwarf reluctantly drained the beaker. 'See what a glass of good wine can do! Why, your eyes are shining already!'

Poor fellow! his large eyes *gleamed*, rather than shone; for the effect of wine on his excitable brain was not more powerful than instantaneous. He placed the goblet nervously on the table, and looked round upon the company with a half-insane stare. They all seemed highly amused at the success of the king's '*joke*'.

'And now to business,' said the prime minister, a *very* fat man.

'Yes,' said the king. 'Come, Hop-Frog, lend us your assistance. Characters, my fine fellow; we stand in need of characters – all of us – ha! ha! ha!' and as this was seriously meant for a joke, his laugh was chorused by the seven.

Hop-Frog also laughed, although feebly and somewhat vacantly.

'Come, come,' said the king, impatiently, 'have you nothing to suggest?'

'I am endeavoring to think of something *novel*,' replied the dwarf, abstractedly, for he was quite bewildered by the wine.

'Endeavoring!' cried the tyrant, fiercely; 'what do you mean by *that*? Ah, I perceive. You are sulky, and want more wine. Here, drink this!' and he poured out another goblet full and offered it to the cripple, who merely gazed at it, gasping for breath.

'Drink, I say!' shouted the monster, 'or by the fiends –'

The dwarf hesitated. The king grew purple with rage. The courtiers smirked. Trippetta, pale as a corpse, advanced to the monarch's seat, and, falling on her knees before him, implored him to spare her friend.

The tyrant regarded her, for some moments, in evident wonder at her audacity. He seemed quite at a loss what to do or say – how most becomingly to express his indignation. At last, without uttering a syllable, he pushed her violently from him, and threw the contents of the brimming goblet in her face.

The poor girl got up as best she could, and, not daring even to sigh, resumed her position at the foot of the table.

There was a dead silence for about half a minute, during which the falling of a leaf, or of a feather, might have been heard. It was interrupted by a low, but harsh and protracted *grating* sound which seemed to come at once from every corner of the room.

'What – what – *what* are you making that noise for?' demanded the king, turning furiously to the dwarf.

The latter seemed to have recovered, in great measure, from his intoxication, and looking fixedly but quietly in the tyrant's face, merely ejaculated:

'I – I? How could it have been me?'

'The sound appeared to come from without,' observed one of the courtiers. 'I fancy it was the parrot at the window, whetting his bill upon his cage-wires.'

'True,' replied the monarch, as if much relieved

by the suggestion; 'but, on the honor of a knight, I could have sworn that it was the gritting of this vagabond's teeth.'

Hereupon the dwarf laughed (the king was too confirmed a joker to object to any one's laughing), and displayed a set of large, powerful, and very repulsive teeth. Moreover, he avowed his perfect willingness to swallow as much wine as desired. The monarch was pacified; and having drained another bumper with no very perceptible ill effect, Hop-Frog entered at once, and with spirit, into the plans for the masquerade.

'I cannot tell what was the association of idea,' observed he, very tranquilly, and as if he had never tasted wine in his life, 'but *just after* your majesty had struck the girl and thrown the wine in her face – *just after* your majesty had done this, and while the parrot was making that odd noise outside the window, there came into my mind a capital diversion – one of my own country frolics – often enacted among us, at our masquerades; but here it will be new altogether. Unfortunately, however, it requires a company of eight persons, and –'

'Here we *are*!' cried the king, laughing at his acute discovery of the coincidence; 'eight to a fraction – I and my seven ministers. Come! what is the diversion?'

'We call it,' replied the cripple, 'the Eight Chained Ourang-Outangs, and it really is excellent sport if well enacted.'

'*We* will enact it,' remarked the king, drawing himself up, and lowering his eyelids.

'The beauty of the game,' continued Hop-Frog, 'lies in the fright it occasions among the women.'

'Capital!' roared in chorus the monarch and his ministry.

'I will equip you as ourang-outangs,' proceeded the dwarf; 'leave all that to me. The resemblance shall be so striking, that the company of masqueraders will take you for real beasts – and of course, they will be as much terrified as astonished.'

'Oh, this is exquisite!' exclaimed the king. 'Hop-Frog! I will make a man of you.'

'The chains are for the purpose of increasing the confusion by their jangling. You are supposed to have escaped, *en masse*, from your keepers. Your majesty cannot conceive the *effect* produced, at a masquerade, by eight chained ourang-outangs, imagined to be real ones by most of the company; and rushing in with savage cries, among the crowd of delicately and gorgeously habited men and women. The *contrast* is inimitable.'

'It *must* be,' said the king: and the council arose hurriedly (as it was growing late), to put in execution the scheme of Hop-Frog.

His mode of equipping the party as ourang-outangs was very simple, but effective enough for his purposes. The animals in question had, at the epoch of my story, very rarely been seen in any part of the civilized world; and as the imitations made by the dwarf were sufficiently beast-like and more than sufficiently hideous, their truthfulness to nature was thus thought to be secured.

The king and his ministers were first encased in tight-fitting stockinet shirts and drawers. They were then saturated with tar. At this stage of the process, some one of the party suggested feathers; but the suggestion was at once overruled by the dwarf, who soon convinced the eight, by ocular demonstration, that the hair of such a brute as the ourang-outang was much more efficiently represented by *flax*. A thick coating of the latter was accordingly plastered upon the coating of tar. A long chain was now procured. First, it was passed about the waist of the king, *and tied*; then about another of the party, and also tied; then about all successively, in the same manner. When this chaining arrangement was complete, and the party stood as far apart from each other as possible, they formed a circle; and to make all things appear natural, Hop-Frog passed the residue of the chain, in two diameters, at right angles, across the circle, after the fashion adopted, at the present day, by those who capture chimpanzees, or other large apes, in Borneo.

The grand saloon in which the masquerade was to take place, was a circular room, very lofty, and receiving the light of the sun only through a single window at top. At night (the season for which the apartment was especially designed) it was illuminated principally by a large chandelier, depending by a chain from the centre of the skylight, and lowered, or elevated, by means of a counterbalance as usual; but (in order not to look unsightly) this latter passed outside the cupola and over the roof.

The arrangements of the room had been left to Trippetta's superintendence; but, in some particulars, it seems, she had been guided by the calmer judgment of her friend the dwarf. At his suggestion it was that, on this occasion, the chandelier was removed. Its waxen drippings (which, in weather so warm, it was quite impossible to prevent) would have been seriously detrimental to the rich dresses of the guests, who, on account of the crowded state of the saloon, could not *all* be expected to keep from out its centre – that is to say, from under the chandelier. Additional sconces were set in various parts of the hall, out of the way; and a flambeau, emitting sweet odor, was placed in the right hand of each of the Caryatides that stood against the wall – some fifty or sixty all together.

The eight ourang-outangs, taking Hop-Frog's advice, waited patiently until midnight (when the room was thoroughly filled with masqueraders) before making their appearance. No sooner had the clock ceased striking, however, than they rushed, or rather rolled in, all together – for the impediments of their chains caused most of the party to fall, and all to stumble as they entered.

The excitement among the masqueraders was prodigious, and filled the heart of the king with glee. As had been anticipated, there were not a few of the guests who supposed the ferocious-looking creatures to be beasts of *some* kind in reality, if not precisely ourang-outangs. Many of the women swooned with affright; and had not the king taken the precaution to exclude all weapons from the saloon, his party might soon have expiated their frolic in their blood. As it was, a general rush was made for the doors; but the king had ordered them to be locked immediately upon his entrance; and, at the dwarf's suggestion, the keys had been deposited with *him*.

While the tumult was at its height, and each masquerader attentive only to his own safety (for, in fact, there was much *real* danger from the pressure of the excited crowd), the chain by which the chandelier ordinarily hung, and which had been drawn up on its removal, might have been seen very gradually to descend, until its hooked extremity came within three feet of the floor.

Soon after this, the king and his seven friends having reeled about the hall in all directions, found themselves, at length, in its centre, and, of course, in immediate contact with the chain. While they were thus situated, the dwarf, who had followed noiselessly at their heels, inciting them to keep up the commotion, took hold of their own chain at the intersection of the two portions which crossed the circle diametrically and at right angles. Here, with the rapidity of thought, he inserted the hook from which the chandelier had been wont to depend; and, in an instant, by some unseen agency, the chandelier-chain was drawn so far upward as to take the hook out of reach, and, as an inevitable consequence, to drag the ourang-outangs together in close connection, and face to face.

The masqueraders, by this time, had recovered, in some measure, from their alarm; and, beginning to regard the whole matter as a well-contrived pleasantry, set up a loud shout of laughter at the predicament of the apes.

'Leave them to *me*!' now screamed Hop-Frog, his shrill voice making itself easily heard through all the din. 'Leave them to *me*. I fancy *I* know them. If I can only get a good look at them, *I* can soon tell who they are.'

Here, scrambling over the heads of the crowd, he managed to get to the wall; when, seizing a flambeau from one of the Caryatides, he returned, as he went, to the centre of the room – leaped, with the agility of a monkey, upon the king's head – and thence clambered a few feet up the chain – holding down the torch to examine the group of ourang-outangs, and still screaming: '*I* shall soon find out who they are!'

And now, while the whole assembly (the apes included) were convulsed with laughter, the jester suddenly uttered a shrill whistle; when the chain flew violently up for about thirty feet – dragging with it the dismayed and struggling ourang-outangs, and leaving them suspended in mid-air between the skylight and the floor. Hop-Frog, clinging to the chain as it rose, still maintained his relative position in respect to the eight maskers, and still (as if nothing were the matter) continued to thrust his torch down toward them, as though endeavoring to discover who they were.

So thoroughly astonished was the whole company at this ascent, that a dead silence, of about a minute's duration, ensued. It was broken by just such a low, harsh, *grating* sound, as had before attracted the attention of the king and his councillors when the former threw the wine in the face of Trippetta. But, on the present occasion, there could be no question as to *whence* the sound issued. It came from the fang-like teeth of the dwarf who ground them and gnashed them as he foamed at the mouth, and glared, with an expression of maniacal rage, into the upturned countenances of the king and his seven companions.

'Ah, ha!' said at length the infuriated jester. 'Ah, ha! I begin to see who these people *are* now!' Here, pretending to scrutinize the king more closely, he held the flambeau to the flaxen coat which enveloped him, and which instantly burst into a sheet of vivid flame. In less than half a minute the whole eight ourang-outangs were blazing fiercely, amid the shrieks of the multitude who gazed at them from below, horror-stricken, and without the power to render them the slightest assistance.

At length the flames, suddenly increasing in

virulence, forced the jester to climb higher up the chain, to be out of their reach; and, as he made this movement, the crowd again sank, for a brief instant, into silence. The dwarf seized his opportunity, and once more spoke:

'I now see *distinctly*,' he said, 'what manner of people these maskers are. They are a great king and his seven privy-councillors – a king who does not scruple to strike a defenceless girl, and his seven councillors who abet him in the outrage. As for myself, I am simply Hop-Frog, the jester – and *this is my last jest*.'

Owing to the high combustibility of both the flax and the tar to which it adhered, the dwarf had scarcely made an end of his brief speech before the work of vengeance was complete. The eight corpses swung in their chains, a fetid, blackened, hideous, and indistinguishable mass. The cripple hurled his torch at them, clambered leisurely to the ceiling, and disappeared through the skylight.

It is supposed that Trippetta, stationed on the roof of the saloon, had been the accomplice of her friend in his fiery revenge, and that, together, they effected their escape to their own country; for neither was seen again.

SOME WORDS WITH A MUMMY

The *symposium* of the preceding evening had been a little too much for my nerves. I had a wretched headache, and was desperately drowsy. Instead of going out, therefore, to spend the evening, as I had proposed, it occurred to me that I could not do a wiser thing than just eat a mouthful of supper and go immediately to bed.

A *light* supper, of course. I am exceedingly fond of Welsh-rabbit. More than a pound at once, however, may not at all times be advisable. Still, there can be no material objection to two. And really between two and three, there is merely a single unit of difference. I ventured, perhaps, upon four. My wife will have it five; but, clearly, she has confounded two very distinct affairs. The abstract number, five, I am willing to admit; but, concretely, it has reference to bottles of Brown Stout, without which, in the way of condiment, Welsh-rabbit is to be eschewed.

Having thus concluded a frugal meal, and donned my nightcap, with the sincere hope of enjoying it till noon the next day, I placed my head upon the pillow, and, through the aid of a capital conscience, fell into a profound slumber forthwith.

But when were the hopes of humanity fulfilled? I could not have completed my third snore when there came a furious ringing at the street-door bell, and then an impatient thumping at the knocker, which awakened me at once. In a minute afterward, and while I was still rubbing my eyes, my wife thrust in my face a note, from my old friend, Doctor Ponnonner. It ran thus:

Come to me, by all means, my dear good friend, as soon as you receive this. Come and help us to rejoice. At last, by long persevering diplomacy, I have gained the assent of the Directors of the City Museum, to my examination of the Mummy – you know the one I mean. I have permission to unswathe it and open it, if desirable. A few friends only will be present – you, of course. The Mummy is now at my house, and we shall begin to unroll it at eleven tonight.

Yours, ever,
PONNONNER

By the time I had reached the 'Ponnonner', it struck me that I was as wide awake as a man need be. I leaped out of bed in an ecstasy, overthrowing all in my way; dressed myself with a rapidity truly marvellous; and set off, at the top of my speed, for the Doctor's.

There I found a very eager company assembled. They had been awaiting me with much impatience; the Mummy was extended upon the dining-table; and the moment I entered its examination was commenced.

It was one of a pair brought, several years previously, by Captain Arthur Sabretash, a cousin of Ponnonner's, from a tomb near Eleithias, in the Libyan mountains, a considerable distance above Thebes on the Nile. The grottos at this point, although less magnificent than the Theban sepulchres, are of higher interest, on account of affording more numerous illustrations of the private life of the Egyptians. The chamber from which our specimen was taken, was said to be very rich in such illustrations – the walls being completely covered with fresco paintings and bas-reliefs, while statues, vases, and mosaic work of rich patterns, indicated the vast wealth of the deceased.

The treasure had been deposited in the museum precisely in the same condition in which Captain Sabretash had found it – that is to say, the coffin had not been disturbed. For eight years it had thus stood, subject only externally to public inspection. We had now, therefore, the complete Mummy at our disposal; and to those who are aware how very rarely the unransacked antique reaches our shores, it will be evident, at once, that we had great reason to congratulate ourselves upon our good fortune.

Approaching the table, I saw on it a large box, or case, nearly seven feet long, and perhaps three feet wide, by two feet and a half deep. It was oblong – not coffin-shaped. The material was at first supposed to be the wood of the sycamore (*platanus*), but, upon cutting into it, we found it to be pasteboard, or, more properly, *papier mâché*, composed of papyrus. It was thickly ornamented with paintings, representing funeral scenes, and other mournful subjects – interspersed among which, in every variety of position, were certain series of hieroglyphical characters, intended, no doubt, for the name of the departed. By good luck, Mr Gliddon formed one of our party; and he had no difficulty in translating the letters, which were simply phonetic, and represented the word, *Allamistakeo*.

We had some difficulty in getting this case open without injury; but, having at length accomplished the task, we came to a second, coffin-shaped, and very considerably less in size than the exterior one, but resembling it precisely in every other respect. The interval between the two was filled with resin, which had, in some degree, defaced the colors of the interior box.

Upon opening this latter (which we did quite easily), we arrived at a third case, also coffin-shaped, and varying from the second one in no particular, except in that of its material, which was cedar, and still emitted the peculiar and highly aromatic odor of that wood. Between the second and the third case there was no interval – the one fitting accurately within the other.

Removing the third case, we discovered and

took out the body itself. We had expected to find it, as usual, enveloped in frequent rolls, or bandages, of linen; but, in place of these, we found a sort of sheath, made of papyrus, and coated with a layer of plaster, thickly gilt and painted. The paintings represented subjects connected with the various supposed duties of the soul, and its presentation to different divinities, with numerous identical human figures, intended, very probably, as portraits of the persons embalmed. Extending from head to foot was a columnar, or perpendicular, inscription, in phonetic hieroglyphics, giving again his name and titles, and the names and titles of his relations.

Around the neck thus unsheathed, was a collar of cylindrical glass beads, diverse in color, and so arranged as to form images of deities, of the scarabaeus, etc., with the winged globe. Around the small of the waist was a similar collar or belt.

Stripping off the papyrus, we found the flesh in excellent preservation, with no perceptible odor. The color was reddish. The skin was hard, smooth, and glossy. The teeth and hair were in good condition. The eyes (it seemed) had been removed, and glass ones substituted, which were very beautiful and wonderfully life-like, with the exception of somewhat too determined a stare. The fingers and the nails were brilliantly gilded.

Mr Gliddon was of opinion, from the redness of the epidermis, that the embalmment had been effected altogether by asphaltum; but, on scraping the surface with a steel instrument, and throwing into the fire some of the powder thus obtained, the flavor of camphor and other sweet-scented gums became apparent.

We searched the corpse very carefully for the usual openings through which the entrails are extracted, but, to our surprise, we could discover none. No member of the party was at that period aware that entire or unopened mummies are not unfrequently met. The brain it was customary to withdraw through the nose; the intestines through an incision in the side; the body was then shaved, washed, and salted; then, laid aside for several weeks, when the operation of embalming, properly so called, began.

As no trace of an opening could be found, Doctor Ponnonner was preparing his instruments for dissection, when I observed that it was then past two o'clock. Hereupon it was agreed to postpone the internal examination until the next evening; and we were about to separate for the present, when someone suggested an experiment or two with the Voltaic pile.

The application of electricity to a Mummy three or four thousand years old at the least, was an idea, if not very sage, still sufficiently original, and we all caught it at once. About one tenth in earnest and nine tenths in jest, we arranged a battery in the Doctor's study, and conveyed thither the Egyptian.

It was only after much trouble that we succeeded in laying bare some portions of the temporal muscle which appeared of less stony rigidity than other parts of the frame, but which, as we had anticipated, of course, gave no indication of galvanic susceptibility when brought in contact with the wire. This, the first trial, indeed, seemed decisive, and, with a hearty laugh at our own absurdity, we were bidding each other good night, when my eyes, happening to fall upon those of the Mummy, were there immediately riveted in amazement. My brief glance, in fact, had sufficed to assure me that the orbs which we had all supposed to be glass, and which were originally noticeable for a certain wild stare, were now so far covered by the lids, that only a small portion of the *tunica albuginea* remained visible.

With a shout I called attention to the fact, and it became immediately obvious to all.

I cannot say that I was *alarmed* at the phenomenon, because 'alarmed' is, in my case, not exactly the word. It is possible, however, that, but for the Brown Stout, I might have been a little nervous. As for the rest of the company, they really made no attempt at concealing the downright fright which possessed them. Doctor Ponnonner was a man to be pitied. Mr Gliddon, by some peculiar process, rendered himself invisible. Mr Silk Buckingham, I fancy, will scarcely be so bold as to deny that he made his way, upon all fours, under the table.

After the first shock of astonishment, however,

we resolved, as a matter of course, upon further experiment forthwith. Our operations were now directed against the great toe of the right foot. We made an incision over the outside of the exterior *os sesamoideum pollicis pedis*, and thus got at the root of the *abductor* muscle. Readjusting the battery, we now applied the fluid to the bisected nerves – when, with a movement of exceeding life-likeness, the Mummy first drew up its right knee so as to bring it nearly in contact with the abdomen, and then, straightening the limb with inconceivable force, bestowed a kick upon Doctor Ponnonner, which had the effect of discharging that gentleman, like an arrow from a catapult, through a window into the street below.

We rushed out *en masse* to bring in the mangled remains of the victim, but had the happiness to meet him upon the staircase, coming up in an unaccountable hurry, brimful of the most ardent philosophy, and more than ever impressed with the necessity of prosecuting our experiment with vigor and with zeal.

It was by his advice, accordingly, that we made, upon the spot, a profound incision into the tip of the subject's nose, while the Doctor himself laying violent hands upon it, pulled it into vehement contact with the wire.

Morally and physically – figuratively and literally – was the effect electric. In the first place, the corpse opened its eyes and winked very rapidly for several minutes as does Mr Barnes in the pantomime; in the second place, it sneezed; in the third, it sat upon end; in the fourth, it shook its fist in Doctor Ponnonner's face; in the fifth, turning to Messieurs Gliddon and Buckingham, it addressed them, in very capital Egyptian, thus:

'I must say, gentlemen, that I am as much surprised as I am mortified at your behavior. Of Doctor Ponnonner nothing better was to be expected. He is a poor little fat fool who *knows* no better. I pity and forgive him. But you, Mr Gliddon – and you, Silk – who have travelled and resided in Egypt until one might imagine you to the manor born – you, I say, who have been so much among us that you speak Egyptian fully as well, I think, as you write your mother-tongue – you, whom I have always been led to regard as the firm friend of the mummies – I really did anticipate more gentlemanly conduct from *you*. What am I to think of your standing quietly by and seeing me thus unhandsomely used? What am I to suppose by your permitting Tom, Dick, and Harry to strip me of my coffins, and my clothes, in this wretchedly cold climate? In what light (to come to the point) am I to regard your aiding and abetting that miserable little villain, Doctor Ponnonner, in pulling me by the nose?'

It will be taken for granted, no doubt, that upon hearing this speech under the circumstances, we all either made for the door, or fell into violent hysterics, or went off in a general swoon. One of these three things was, I say, to be expected.

Indeed each and all of these lines of conduct might have been very plausibly pursued. And, upon my word, I am at a loss to know how or why it was that we pursued neither the one nor the other. But, perhaps, the true reason is to be sought in the spirit of the age, which proceeds by the rule of contraries altogether, and is now usually admitted as the solution of everything in the way of paradox and impossibility. Or, perhaps, after all, it was only the Mummy's exceedingly natural and matter-of-course air that divested his words of the terrible. However this may be, the facts are clear, and no member of our party betrayed any very particular trepidation, or seemed to consider that anything had gone very especially wrong.

For my part I was convinced it was all right, and merely stepped aside, out of the range of the Egyptian's fist. Doctor Ponnonner thrust his hands into his breeches' pockets, looked hard at the Mummy, and grew excessively red in the face. Mr Gliddon stroked his whiskers and drew up the collar of his shirt. Mr Buckingham hung down his head, and put his right thumb into the left corner of his mouth.

The Egyptian regarded him with a severe countenance for some minutes, and at length, with a sneer, said:

'Why don't you speak, Mr Buckingham? Did you hear what I asked you, or not? *Do* take your thumb out of your mouth!'

Mr Buckingham, hereupon, gave a slight start,

took his right thumb out of the left corner of his mouth, and, by way of indemnification, inserted his left thumb in the right corner of the aperture above-mentioned.

Not being able to get an answer from Mr B., the figure turned peevishly to Mr Gliddon, and, in a peremptory tone, demanded in general terms what we all meant.

Mr Gliddon replied at great length, in phonetics; and but for the deficiency of American printing-offices in hieroglyphical type, it would afford me much pleasure to record here, in the original, the whole of his very excellent speech.

I may as well take this occasion to remark, that all the subsequent conversation in which the Mummy took a part, was carried on in primitive Egyptian, through the medium (so far as concerned myself and other untravelled members of the company) – through the medium, I say, of Messieurs Gliddon and Buckingham, as interpreters. These gentlemen spoke the mother tongue of the Mummy with inimitable fluency and grace; but I could not help observing that (owing, no doubt, to the introduction of images entirely modern and, of course, entirely novel to the stranger) the two travellers were reduced, occasionally, to the employment of sensible forms for the purpose of conveying a particular meaning. Mr Gliddon, at one period, for example, could not make the Egyptian comprehend the term 'politics', until he sketched upon the wall, with a bit of charcoal, a little carbuncle-nosed gentleman, out at elbows, standing upon a stump, with his left leg drawn back, his right arm thrown forward, with his fist shut, the eyes rolled up toward Heaven, and the mouth open at an angle of ninety degrees. just in the same way Mr Buckingham failed to convey the absolutely modern idea, 'whig', until (at Doctor Ponnonner's suggestion) he grew very pale in the face, and consented to take off his own.

It will be readily understood that Mr Gliddon's discourse turned chiefly upon the vast benefits accruing to science from the unrolling and disembowelling of mummies; apologizing, upon this score, for any disturbance that might have been occasioned *him*, in particular, the individual Mummy called Allamistakeo; and concluding with a mere hint (for it could scarcely be considered more) that, as these little matters were now explained, it might be as well to proceed with the investigation intended. Here Doctor Ponnonner made ready his instruments.

In regard to the latter suggestions of the orator, it appears that Allamistakeo had certain scruples of conscience, the nature of which I did not distinctly learn; but he expressed himself satisfied with the apologies tendered, and, getting down from the table, shook hands with the company all round.

When this ceremony was at an end, we immediately busied ourselves in repairing the damages which our subject had sustained from the scalpel. We sewed up the wound in his temple, bandaged his foot, and applied a square inch of black plaster to the tip of his nose.

It was now observed that the Count (this was the title, it seems, of Allamistakeo) had a slight fit of shivering – no doubt from the cold. The Doctor immediately repaired to his wardrobe, and soon returned with a black dress coat, made in Jennings' best manner, a pair of sky-blue plaid pantaloons with straps, a pink gingham *chemise*, a flapped vest of brocade, a white sack overcoat, a walking cane with a hook, a hat with no brim, patent-leather boots, straw-colored kid gloves, an eye-glass, a pair of whiskers, and a waterfall cravat. Owing to the disparity of size between the Count and the Doctor (the proportion being as two to one), there was some little difficulty in adjusting these habiliments upon the person of the Egyptian; but when all was arranged, he might have been said to be dressed. Mr Gliddon, therefore, gave him his arm, and led him to a comfortable chair by the fire, while the Doctor rang the bell upon the spot and ordered a supply of cigars and wine.

The conversation soon grew animated. Much curiosity was, of course, expressed in regard to the somewhat remarkable fact of Allamistakeo's still remaining alive.

'I should have thought,' observed Mr Buckingham, 'that it is high time you were dead.'

'Why,' replied the Count, very much astonished, 'I am little more than seven hundred years old! My father lived a thousand, and was by no means in his dotage when he died.'

Here ensued a brisk series of questions and computations, by means of which it became evident that the antiquity of the Mummy had been grossly misjudged. It had been five thousand and fifty years and some months since he had been consigned to the catacombs at Eleithias.

'But my remark,' resumed Mr Buckingham, 'had no reference to your age at the period of interment (I am willing to grant, in fact, that you are still a young man), and my allusion was to the immensity of time during which, by your own showing, you must have been done up in asphaltum.'

'In what?' said the Count.

'In asphaltum,' persisted Mr B.

'Ah, yes; I have some faint notion of what you mean; it might be made to answer, no doubt – but in my time we employed scarcely anything else than the Bichloride of Mercury.'

'But what we are especially at a loss to understand,' said Doctor Ponnonner, 'is how it happens that, having been dead and buried in Egypt five thousand years ago, you are here today all alive and looking so delightfully well.'

'Had I been, as you say, *dead*,' replied the Count, 'it is more than probable that dead I should still be; for I perceive you are yet in the infancy of

Galvanism, and cannot accomplish with it what was a common thing among us in the old days. But the fact is, I fell into catalepsy, and it was considered by my best friends that I was either dead or should be; they accordingly embalmed me at once – I presume you are aware of the chief principle of the embalming process?'

'Why, not altogether.'

'Ah, I perceive; a deplorable condition of ignorance! Well, I cannot enter into details just now: but it is necessary to explain that to embalm (properly speaking), in Egypt, was to arrest indefinitely *all* the animal functions subjected to the process. I use the word "animal" in its widest sense, as including the physical not more than the moral and *vital* being. I repeat that the leading principle of embalmment consisted, with us, in the immediately arresting, and holding in perpetual *abeyance,* *all* the animal functions subjected to the process. To be brief, in whatever condition the individual was, at the period of embalmment, in that condition he remained. Now, as it is my good fortune to be of the blood of the Scarabaeus, I was embalmed *alive*, as you see me at present.'

'The blood of the Scarabaeus!' exclaimed Doctor Ponnonner.

'Yes. The Scarabaeus was the *insignium*, or the "arms", of a very distinguished and very rare patrician family. To be "of the blood of the Scarabaeus", is merely to be one of that family of which the Scarabaeus is the *insignium*. I speak figuratively.'

'But what has this to do with your being alive?'

'Why, it is the general custom in Egypt to deprive a corpse, before embalmment, of its bowels and brains; the race of the Scarabaei alone did not coincide with the custom. Had I not been a Scarabaeus, therefore, I should have been without bowels and brains; and without either it is inconvenient to live.'

'I perceive that,' said Mr Buckingham, 'and I presume that all the *entire* mummies that come to hand are of the race of Scarabaei.'

'Beyond doubt.'

'I thought,' said Mr Gliddon, very meekly, 'that the Scarabaeus was one of the Egyptian gods.'

'One of the Egyptian *what?*' exclaimed the Mummy, starting to its feet.

'Gods!' repeated the traveller.

'Mr Gliddon, I really am astonished to hear you talk in this style,' said the Count, resuming his chair. 'No nation upon the face of the earth has ever acknowledged more than *one god*. The Scarabaeus, the Ibis, etc., were with us (as similar creatures have been with others) the symbols, or *media*, through which we offered worship to the Creator too august to be more directly approached.'

There was here a pause. At length the colloquy was renewed by Doctor Ponnonner.

'It is not improbable, then, from what you have

explained,' said he, 'that among the catacombs near the Nile there may exist other mummies of the Scarabaeus tribe, in a condition of vitality.'

'There can be no question of it,' replied the Count; 'all the Scarabaei embalmed accidentally while alive, are alive. Even some of those *purposely* so embalmed, may have been overlooked by their executors, and still remain in the tomb.'

'Will you be kind enough to explain,' I said, 'what you mean by "purposely so embalmed"?'

'With great pleasure,' answered the Mummy, after surveying me leisurely through his eye-glass – for it was the first time I had ventured to address him a direct question.

'With great pleasure,' he said. 'The usual duration of man's life, in my time, was about eight hundred years. Few men died, unless by most extraordinary accident, before the age of six hundred; few lived longer than a decade of centuries; but eight were considered the natural term. After the discovery of the embalming principle, as I have already described it to you, it occurred to our philosophers that a laudable curiosity might be gratified, and, at the same time, the interests of science much advanced, by living this natural term in instalments. In the case of history, indeed, experience demonstrated that something of this kind was indispensable. An historian, for example, having attained the age of five hundred, would write a book with great labor and then get himself carefully embalmed; leaving instructions to his executors *pro tem.*, that they should cause him to be revivified after the lapse of a certain period – say five or six hundred years. Resuming existence at the expiration of this time, he would invariably find his great work converted into a species of haphazard notebook – that is to say, into a kind of literary arena for the conflicting guesses, riddles, and personal squabbles of whole herds of exasperated commentators. These guesses, etc., which passed under the name of annotations, or emendations, were found so completely to have enveloped, distorted, and overwhelmed the text, that the author had to go about with a lantern to discover his own book. When discovered, it was never worth the trouble of the search. After rewriting it throughout, it was regarded as the bounden duty of the historian to set himself to work immediately in correcting, from his own private knowledge and experience, the traditions of the day concerning the epoch at which he had originally lived. Now this process of rescription and personal rectification, pursued by various individual sages from time to time, had the effect of preventing our history from degenerating into absolute fable.'

'I beg your pardon,' said Doctor Ponnonner at this point, laying his hand gently upon the arm of the Egyptian – 'I beg your pardon, sir, but may I presume to interrupt you for one moment?'

'By all means, *sir*,' replied the Count, drawing up.

'I merely wished to ask you a question,' said the

Doctor. 'You mentioned the historian's personal correction of *traditions* respecting his own epoch. Pray, sir, upon an average, what proportion of these Kabbala were usually found to be right?'

'The Kabbala, as you properly term them, sir, were generally discovered to be precisely on a par with the facts recorded in the un-rewritten histories themselves; that is to say, not one individual iota of either was ever known, under any circumstances, to be not totally and radically wrong.'

'But since it is quite clear,' resumed the Doctor, 'that at least five thousand years have elapsed since your entombment, I take it for granted that your histories at that period, if not your traditions, were sufficiently explicit on that one topic of universal interest, the Creation, which took place, as I presume you are aware, only about ten centuries before.'

'Sir!' said the Count Allamistakeo.

The Doctor repeated his remarks, but it was only after much additional explanation that the foreigner could be made to comprehend them. The latter at length said, hesitatingly:

'The ideas you have suggested are to me, I confess, utterly novel. During my time I never knew anyone to entertain so singular a fancy as that the universe (or this world if you will have it so) ever had a beginning at all. I remember once, and once only, hearing something remotely hinted, by a man of many speculations, concerning the origin *of the human race*; and by this individual, the very word *Adam* (or Red Earth), which you make use of, was employed. He employed it, however, in a generical sense, with reference to the spontaneous germination from rank soil (just as a thousand of the lower *genera* of creatures are germinated), the spontaneous germination, I say, of five vast hordes of men, simultaneously upspringing in five distinct and nearly equal divisions of the globe.'

Here, in general, the company shrugged their shoulders, and one or two of us touched our foreheads with a very significant air. Mr Silk Buckingham, first glancing slightly at the occiput and then at the sinciput of Allamistakeo, spoke as follows:

'The long duration of human life in your time, together with the occasional practice of passing it, as you have explained, in instalments, must have had, indeed, a strong tendency to the general development and conglomeration of knowledge. I presume, therefore, that we are to attribute the marked inferiority of the old Egyptians in all particulars of science, when compared with the moderns, and more especially with the Yankees, altogether to the superior solidity of the Egyptian skull.'

'I confess again,' replied the Count, with much suavity, 'that I am somewhat at a loss to comprehend you; pray, to what particulars of science do you allude?'

Here our whole party, joining voices, detailed,

at great length, the assumptions of phrenology and the marvels of animal magnetism.

Having heard us to an end, the Count proceeded to relate a few anecdotes, which rendered it evident that prototypes of Gall and Spurzheim had flourished and faded in Egypt so long ago as to have been nearly forgotten, and that the manoeuvres of Mesmer were really very contemptible tricks when put in collation with the positive miracles of the Theban *savants*, who created lice and a great many other similar things.

I here asked the Count if his people were able to calculate eclipses. He smiled rather contemptuously, and said they were.

This put me a little out, but I began to make other inquiries in regard to his astronomical knowledge, when a member of the company, who had never as yet opened his mouth, whispered in my ear, that for information on this head, I had better consult Ptolemy (whoever Ptolemy is), as well as one Plutarch *de facie lunae*.

I then questioned the Mummy about burning-glasses and lenses, and, in general, about the manufacture of glass; but I had not made an end of my queries before the silent member again touched me quietly on the elbow, and begged me for God's sake to take a peep at Diodorus Siculus. As for the Count, he merely asked me, in the way of reply, if we moderns possessed any such microscopes as would enable us to cut cameos in the style of the Egyptians. While I was thinking how

I should answer this question, little Doctor Pon-nonner committed himself in a very extraordinary way.

'Look at our architecture!' he exclaimed, greatly to the indignation of both the travellers, who pinched him black and blue to no purpose.

'Look,' he cried with enthusiasm, 'at the Bowling-Green Fountain in New York! or if this be too vast a contemplation, regard for the moment the Capitol at Washington, DC!' – and the good little medical man went on to detail, very minutely, the proportions of the fabric to which he referred. He explained that the portico alone was adorned with no less than four and twenty columns, five feet in diameter, and ten feet apart.

The Count said that he regretted not being able to remember, just at that moment, the precise dimensions of any one of the principal buildings of the city of Aznac, whose foundations were laid in the night of Time, but the ruins of which were still standing, at the epoch of his entombment, in a vast plain of sand to the westward of Thebes. He recollected, however (talking of the porticos) that one affixed to an inferior palace in a kind of suburb called Carnac, consisted of a hundred and forty-four columns, thirty-seven feet in circumfer-ence, and twenty-five feet apart. The approach to this portico, from the Nile, was through an avenue two miles long, composed of sphynxes, statues, and obelisks, twenty, sixty, and a hundred feet in height. The palace itself (as well as he could remember) was, in one direction, two miles long, and might have been altogether about seven in circuit. Its walls were richly painted all over, within and without, with hieroglyphics. He would not pretend to *assert* that even fifty or sixty of the Doctor's Capitols might have been built within these walls, but he was by no means sure that two or three hundred of them might not have been squeezed in with some trouble. That palace at Carnac was an insignificant little building after all. He (the Count), however, could not conscientiously refuse to admit the ingenuity, magnificence, and superiority of the Fountain at the Bowling Green, as described by the Doctor. Nothing like it, he was forced to allow, had ever been seen in Egypt or elsewhere.

I here asked the Count what he had to say to our railroads.

'Nothing,' he replied, 'in particular.' They were rather slight, rather ill-conceived, and clumsily put together. They could not be compared, of course, with the vast, level, direct, iron-grooved causeways upon which the Egyptians conveyed entire temples and solid obelisks of a hundred and fifty feet in altitude.

I spoke of our gigantic mechanical forces.

He agreed that we knew something in that way, but inquired how I should have gone to work in getting up the imposts on the lintels of even the little palace at Carnac.

This question I concluded not to hear, and

demanded if he had any idea of Artesian wells; but he simply raised his eyebrows; while Mr Gliddon winked at me very hard and said, in a low tone, that one had been recently discovered by the engineers employed to bore for water in the Great Oasis.

I then mentioned our steel; but the foreigner elevated his nose, and asked me if our steel could have executed the sharp carved work seen on the obelisks, and which was wrought altogether by edge-tools of copper.

This disconcerted us so greatly that we thought it advisable to vary the attack to Metaphysics. We sent for a copy of a book called the *Dial* and read out of it a chapter or two about something which is not very clear, but which the Bostonians call the Great Movement of Progress.

The Count merely said that Great Movements were awfully common things in his day, and as for Progress, it was at one time quite a nuisance, but it never progressed.

We then spoke of the great beauty and importance of Democracy, and were at much trouble in impressing the Count with a due sense of the advantages we enjoyed in living where there was suffrage *ad libitum*, and no king.

He listened with marked interest, and in fact seemed not a little amused. When we had done, he said that, a great while ago, there had occurred something of a very similar sort. Thirteen Egyptian provinces determined all at once to be free, and to set a magnificent example to the rest of mankind. They assembled their wise men, and concocted the most ingenious constitution it is possible to conceive. For a while they managed remarkably well; only their habit of bragging was prodigious. The thing ended, however, in the consolidation of the thirteen states, with some fifteen or twenty others, in the most odious and insupportable despotism that was ever heard of upon the face of the Earth.

I asked what was the name of the usurping tyrant.

As well as the Count could recollect, it was *Mob*.

Not knowing what to say to this, I raised my voice, and deplored the Egyptian ignorance of steam.

The Count looked at me with much astonishment, but made no answer. The silent gentleman, however, gave me a violent nudge in the ribs with his elbows – told me I had sufficiently exposed myself for once – and demanded if I was really such a fool as not to know that the modern steam-engine was derived from the invention of Hero, through Solomon de Caus.

We were now in imminent danger of being discomfited; but, as good luck would have it, Doctor Ponnonner, having rallied, returned to our rescue, and inquired if the people of Egypt would seriously pretend to rival the moderns in the all-important particular of dress.

The Count, at this, glanced downward to the

straps of his pantaloons, and then taking hold of the end of one of his coat-tails, held it up close to his eyes for some minutes. Letting it fall, at last, his mouth extended itself very gradually from ear to ear; but I do not remember that he said any thing in the way of reply.

Hereupon we recovered our spirits, and the Doctor, approaching the Mummy with great dignity, desired it to say candidly, upon its honor as a gentleman, if the Egyptians had comprehended, at *any* period, the manufacture of either Ponnonner's lozenges or Brandreth's pills.

We looked, with profound anxiety, for an answer – but in vain. It was not forthcoming. The Egyptian blushed and hung down his head. Never was triumph more consummate; never was defeat borne with so ill a grace. Indeed, I could not endure the spectacle of the poor Mummy's mortification. I reached my hat, bowed to him stiffly, and took leave.

Upon getting home I found it past four o'clock, and went immediately to bed. It is now ten a.m. I have been up since seven, penning these memoranda for the benefit of my family and of mankind. The former I shall behold no more. My wife is a shrew. The truth is, I am heartily sick of this life and of the nineteenth century in general. I am convinced that everything is going wrong. Besides, I am anxious to know who will be President in 2045. As soon, therefore, as I shave and swallow a cup of coffee, I shall just step over to Ponnonner's and get embalmed for a couple of hundred years.

WILLIAM WILSON

What say of it? what say CONSCIENCE grim,
That spectre of my path?

– CHAMBERLAIN's *Pharronida*

Let me call myself, for the present, William
Wilson. The fair page now lying before me need
not be sullied with my real appellation. This has
been already too much an object for the scorn –
for the horror – for the detestation of my race. To
the uttermost regions of the globe have not the
indignant winds bruited its unparalleled infamy?
Oh, outcast of all outcasts most abandoned! – to
the earth art thou not for ever dead? to its honors,
to its flowers, to its golden aspirations? – and a
cloud, dense, dismal, and limitless, does it not
hang eternally between thy hopes and heaven?

I would not, if I could, here or today, embody a
record of my later years of unspeakable misery,
and unpardonable crime. This epoch – these later
years – took unto themselves a sudden elevation in
turpitude, whose origin alone it is my present
purpose to assign. Men usually grow base by

degrees. From me, in an instant, all virtue dropped bodily as a mantle. From comparatively trivial wickedness I passed, with the stride of a giant, into more than the enormities of an Elah-Gabalus. What chance – what one event brought this evil thing to pass, bear with me while I relate. Death approaches; and the shadow which foreruns him has thrown a softening influence over my spirit. I long, in passing through the dim valley, for the sympathy – I had nearly said for the pity – of my fellow men. I would fain have them believe that I have been, in some measure, the slave of circumstances beyond human control. I would wish them to seek out for me, in the details I am about to give, some little oasis of *fatality* amid a wilderness of error. I would have them allow – what they cannot refrain from allowing – that, although temptation may have erewhile existed as great, man was never *thus*, at least, tempted before – certainly, never *thus* fell. And is it therefore that he has never thus suffered? Have I not indeed been living in a dream? And am I not now dying a victim to the horror and the mystery of the wildest of all sublunary visions?

I am the descendant of a race whose imaginative and easily excitable temperament has at all times rendered them remarkable; and, in my earliest infancy, I gave evidence of having fully inherited the family character. As I advanced in years it was more strongly developed; becoming, for many reasons, a cause for serious disquietude to my friends, and of positive injury to myself. I grew self-willed, addicted to the wildest caprices, and a prey to the most ungovernable passions. Weak-minded, and beset with constitutional infirmities akin to my own, my parents could do but little to check the evil propensities which distinguished me. Some feeble and ill-directed efforts resulted in complete failure on their part, and, of course, in total triumph on mine. Thenceforward my voice was a household law; and at an age when few children have abandoned their leading-strings, I was left to the guidance of my own will, and became, in all but name, the master of my own actions.

My earliest recollections of a school-life, are connected with a large, rambling, Elizabethan house, in a misty-looking village of England, where were a vast number of gigantic and gnarled trees, and where all the houses were excessively ancient. In truth, it was a dream-like and spirit-soothing place, that venerable old town. At this moment, in fancy, I feel the refreshing chilliness of its deeply shadowed avenues, inhale the fragrance of its thousand shrubberies, and thrill anew with undefinable delight, at the deep hollow note of the church-bell, breaking, each hour, with sullen and sudden roar, upon the stillness of the dusky atmosphere in which the fretted Gothic steeple lay imbedded and asleep.

It gives me, perhaps, as much of pleasure as I can now in any manner experience, to dwell upon minute recollections of the school and its concerns.

Steeped in misery as I am – misery, alas! only too
real! – I shall be pardoned for seeking relief,
however slight and temporary, in the weakness of
a few rambling details. These, moreover, utterly
trivial, and even ridiculous in themselves, assume,
to my fancy, adventitious importance, as connected with a period and a locality when and
where I recognize the first ambiguous monitions
of the destiny which afterward so fully overshad-
owed me. Let me then remember.

The house, I have said, was old and irregular.
The grounds were extensive, and a high and solid
brick wall, topped with a bed of mortar and broken
glass, encompassed the whole. This prison-like
rampart formed the limit of our domain; beyond
it we saw but thrice a week – once every Saturday
afternoon, when, attended by two ushers, we were
permitted to take brief walks in a body through
some of the neighboring fields – and twice during
Sunday, when we were paraded in the same formal
manner to the morning and evening service in the
one church of the village. Of this church the
principal of our school was pastor. With how deep
a spirit of wonder and perplexity was I wont to
regard him from our remote pew in the gallery,
as, with step solemn and slow, he ascended the
pulpit! This reverend man, with countenance so
demurely benign, with robes so glossy and so
clerically flowing, with wig so minutely powdered,
so rigid and so vast – could this be he who, of
late, with sour visage, and in snuffy habiliments,

administered, ferule in hand, the Draconian Laws of the academy? Oh, gigantic paradox, too utterly monstrous for solution!

At an angle of the ponderous wall frowned a more ponderous gate. It was riveted and studded with iron bolts, and surmounted with jagged iron spikes. What impressions of deep awe did it inspire! It was never opened save for the three periodical egressions and ingressions already mentioned; then, in every creak of its mighty hinges, we found a plenitude of mystery – a world of matter for solemn remark, or for more solemn meditation.

The extensive enclosure was irregular in form, having many capacious recesses. Of these, three or four of the largest constituted the playground. It was level, and covered with fine hard gravel. I well remember it had no trees, nor benches, nor anything similar within it. Of course it was in the rear of the house. In front lay a small parterre, planted with box and other shrubs, but through this sacred division we passed only upon rare occasions indeed – such as a first advent to school or final departure thence, or perhaps, when a parent or friend having called for us, we joyfully took our way home for the Christmas or Midsummer holidays.

But the house! – how quaint an old building was this! – to me how veritably a palace of enchantment! There was really no end to its windings – to its incomprehensible subdivisions. It was difficult,

at any given time, to say with certainty upon
which of its two stories one happened to be. From
each room to every other there were sure to be
found three or four steps either in ascent or descent. Then the lateral branches were innumerable
– inconceivable – and so returning in upon themselves, that our most exact ideas in regard to the
whole mansion were not very far different from
those with which we pondered upon infinity.
During the five years of my residence here, I was
never able to ascertain with precision, in what
remote locality lay the little sleeping apartment
assigned to myself and some eighteen or twenty
other scholars.

The school-room was the largest in the house –
I could not help thinking, in the world. It was
very long, narrow, and dismally low, with pointed
Gothic windows and a ceiling of oak. In a remote
and terror-inspiring angle was a square enclosure
of eight or ten feet, comprising the *sanctum*,
'during hours', of our principal, the Reverend Dr
Bransby. It was a solid structure, with massy
door, sooner than open which, in the absence of
the 'Dominie', we would all have willingly perished by the *peine forte et dure*. In other angles
were two other similar boxes, far less reverenced,
indeed, but still greatly matters of awe. One of
these was the pulpit of the 'classical' usher, one of
the 'English and mathematical'. Interspersed
about the room, crossing and recrossing in endless
irregularity, were innumerable benches and desks,

black, ancient, and time-worn, piled desperately with much bethumbed books, and so beseamed with initial letters, names at full length, grotesque figures, and other multiplied efforts of the knife, as to have entirely lost what little of original form might have been their portion in days long departed. A huge bucket with water stood at one extremity of the room, and a clock of stupendous dimensions at the other.

Encompassed by the massy walls of this venerable academy, I passed, yet not in tedium or disgust, the years of the third lustrum of my life. The teeming brain of childhood requires no external world of incident to occupy or amuse it; and the apparently dismal monotony of a school was replete with more intense excitement than my riper youth has derived from luxury, or my full manhood from crime. Yet I must believe that my first mental development had in it much of the uncommon – even much of the *outré*. Upon mankind at large the events of very early existence rarely leave in mature age any definite impression. All is gray shadow – a weak and irregular remembrance – an indistinct regathering of feeble pleasures and phantasmagoric pains. With me this is not so. In childhood I must have felt with the energy of a man what I now find stamped upon memory in lines as vivid, as deep, and as durable as the *exergues* of the Carthaginian medals.

Yet in fact – in the fact of the world's view – how little was there to remember! The morning's

awakening, the nightly summons to bed; the con-
nings, the recitations; the periodical half-holidays,
and perambulations; the play-ground, with its
broils, its pastimes, its intrigues; these, by a mental
sorcery long forgotten, were made to involve a
wilderness of sensation, a world of rich incident,
an universe of varied emotion, of excitement the
most passionate and spirit-stirring. '*Oh, le bon
temps, que ce siècle de fer!*'

In truth, the ardor, the enthusiasm, and the
imperiousness of my disposition, soon rendered
me a marked character among my schoolmates,
and by slow, but natural gradations, gave me an
ascendency over all not greatly older than myself;
over all with a single exception. This exception
was found in the person of a scholar, who, although no relation, bore the same Christian and
surname as myself: a circumstance, in fact, little
remarkable; for, notwithstanding a noble descent,
mine was one of those everyday appellations which
seem, by prescriptive right, to have been, time out
of mind, the common property of the mob. In this
narrative I have therefore designated myself as
William Wilson, a fictitious title not very dissimi-
lar to the real. My namesake alone, of those who
in school phraseology constituted 'our set', presumed to compete with me in the studies of the
class – in the sports and broils of the playground –
to refuse implicit belief in my assertions, and
submission to my will – indeed, to interfere with
my arbitrary dictation in any respect whatsoever.

If there is on earth a supreme and unqualified despotism, it is the despotism of a mastermind in boyhood over the less energetic spirits of its companions.

Wilson's rebellion was to me a source of the greatest embarrassment; the more so as, in spite of the bravado with which in public I made a point of treating him and his pretensions, I secretly felt that I feared him, and could not help thinking the equality which he maintained so easily with myself, a proof of his true superiority; since not to be overcome, cost me a perpetual struggle. Yet this superiority – even this equality – was in truth acknowledged by no one but myself; our associates, by some unaccountable blindness, seemed not even to suspect it. Indeed, his competition, his resistance, and especially his impertinent and dogged interference with my purposes, were not more pointed than private. He appeared to be destitute alike of the ambition which urged, and of the passionate energy of mind which enabled me to excel. In his rivalry he might have been supposed actuated solely by a whimsical desire to thwart, astonish, or mortify myself; although there were times when I could not help observing, with a feeling made up of wonder, abasement, and pique, that he mingled with his injuries, his insults, or his contradictions, a certain most inappropriate, and assuredly most unwelcome *affectionateness* of manner. I could only conceive this singular behavior to arise from a consummate self-conceit assuming the vulgar airs of patronage and protection.

Perhaps it was this latter trait in Wilson's conduct, conjoined with our identity of name, and the mere accident of our having entered the school upon the same day, which set afloat the notion that we were brothers, among the senior classes in the academy. These do not usually inquire with much strictness into the affairs of their juniors. I have before said, or should have said, that Wilson was not, in a most remote degree, connected with my family. But assuredly if we *had* been brothers we must have been twins; for, after leaving Dr Bransby's, I casually learned that my namesake was born on the nineteenth of January, 1813 – and this is a somewhat remarkable coincidence; for the day is precisely that of my own nativity.

It may seem strange that in spite of the continual anxiety occasioned me by the rivalry of Wilson, and his intolerable spirit of contradiction, I could not bring myself to hate him altogether. We had, to be sure, nearly every day a quarrel in which, yielding me publicly the palm of victory, he, in some manner, contrived to make me feel that it was he who had deserved it; yet a sense of pride on my part, and a veritable dignity on his own, kept us always upon what are called 'speaking terms', while there were many points of strong congeniality in our tempers, operating to awake in me a sentiment which our position alone, perhaps, prevented from ripening into friendship. It is difficult, indeed, to define, or even to describe, my real feelings toward him. They formed a motley and heterogeneous admixture; some petulant animosity, which was not yet hatred, some esteem, more respect, much fear, with a world of uneasy curiosity. To the moralist it will be necessary to say, in addition, that Wilson and myself were the most inseparable of companions.

It was no doubt the anomalous state of affairs existing between us, which turned all my attacks upon him (and there were many, either open or covert) into the channel of banter or practical joke (giving pain while assuming the aspect of mere fun) rather than into a more serious and determined hostility. But my endeavors on this head were by no means uniformly successful, even when my plans were the most wittily concocted; for my namesake had much about him, in character, of that unassuming and quiet austerity which, while enjoying the poignancy of its own jokes, has no heel of Achilles in itself, and absolutely refuses to be laughed at. I could find, indeed, but one vulnerable point, and that, lying in a personal peculiarity, arising, perhaps, from constitutional disease, would have been spared by any antagonist less at his wit's end than myself; my rival had a weakness in the faucial or guttural organs, which precluded him from raising his voice at any time *above a very low whisper*. Of this defect I did not fail to take what poor advantage lay in my power.

Wilson's retaliations in kind were many; and

there was one form of his practical wit that disturbed me beyond measure. How his sagacity first discovered at all that so petty a thing would vex me, is a question I never could solve; but having discovered, he habitually practiced the annoyance. I had always felt aversion to my uncourtly patronymic, and its very common, if not plebeian praenomen. The words were venom in my ears; and when, upon the day of my arrival, a second William Wilson came also to the academy, I felt angry with him for bearing the name, and doubly disgusted with the name because a stranger bore it, who would be the cause of its twofold repetition, who would be constantly in my presence, and whose concerns, in the ordinary routine of the school business, must inevitably, on account of the detestable coincidence, be often confounded with my own.

The feeling of vexation thus engendered grew stronger with every circumstance tending to show resemblance, moral or physical, between my rival and myself. I had not then discovered the remarkable fact that we were of the same age; but I saw that we were of the same height, and I perceived that we were even singularly alike in general contour of person and outline of feature. I was galled, too, by the rumor touching a relationship, which had grown current in the upper forms. In a word, nothing could more seriously disturb me (although I scrupulously concealed such disturbance) than any allusion to a similarity of mind, person, or condition existing between us. But, in truth, I had no reason to believe that (with the exception of the matter of relationship, and in the case of Wilson himself) this similarity had ever been made a subject of comment, or even observed at all by our schoolfellows. That *he* observed it in all its bearings, and as fixedly as I, was apparent; but that he could discover in such circumstances so fruitful a field of annoyance, can only be attributed, as I said before, to his more than ordinary penetration.

His cue, which was to perfect an imitation of myself, lay both in words and in actions; and most admirably did he play his part. My dress it was an easy matter to copy; my gait and general manner were without difficulty, appropriated; in spite of his constitutional defect, even my voice did not escape him. My louder tones were, of course, unattempted, but then the key – it was identical; *and his singular whisper, it grew the very echo of my own.*

How greatly this most exquisite portraiture harassed me (for it could not justly be termed a caricature), I will not now venture to describe. I had but one consolation – in the fact that the imitation, apparently, was noticed by myself alone, and that I had to endure only the knowing and strangely sarcastic smiles of my namesake himself. Satisfied with having produced in my bosom the intended effect, he seemed to chuckle in secret over the sting he had inflicted, and was characteristically disregardful of the public applause which the success of his witty endeavors might have so easily elicited. That the school, indeed, did not feel his design, perceive its accomplishment, and participate in his sneer, was, for many anxious months, a riddle I could not resolve. Perhaps the *gradation* of his copy rendered it not readily perceptible; or, more possibly, I owed my security to the masterly air of the copyist, who, disdaining the letter (which in a painting is all the obtuse can see), gave but the full spirit of his original for my individual contemplation and chagrin.

I have already more than once spoken of the disgusting air of patronage which he assumed toward me, and of his frequent officious interference with my will. This interference often took the ungracious character of advice; advice not openly given, but hinted or insinuated. I received it with a repugnance which gained strength as I grew in years. Yet, at this distant day, let me do him the simple justice to acknowledge that I can recall no occasion when the suggestions of my rival were on the side of those errors or follies so usual to his immature age and seeming inexperience; that his moral sense, at least, if not his general talents and worldly wisdom, was far keener than my own; and that I might, today, have been a better and thus a happier man, had I less frequently rejected the counsels embodied in those meaning whispers which I then but too cordially hated and too bitterly despised.

As it was I at length grew restive in the extreme under his distasteful supervision, and daily resented more and more openly, what I considered his intolerable arrogance. I have said that, in the first years of our connection as schoolmates, my feelings in regard to him might have been easily ripened into friendship; but, in the latter months of my residence at the academy, although the intrusion of his ordinary manner had, beyond doubt, in some measure, abated, my sentiments, in nearly similar proportion, partook very much of positive hatred. Upon one occasion he saw this, I think, and afterward avoided, or made a show of avoiding me.

It was about the same period, if I remember aright, that, in an altercation of violence with him, in which he was more than usually thrown off his guard, and spoke and acted with an openness of demeanor rather foreign to his nature, I discovered, or fancied I discovered, in his accent, in his air, and general appearance, a something which first startled, and then deeply interested me, by bringing to mind dim visions of my earliest infancy – wild, confused, and thronging memories of a time when memory herself was yet unborn. I cannot better describe the sensation which oppressed me, than by saying that I could with difficulty shake off the belief of my having been acquainted with the being who stood before me, at some epoch very long ago – some point of the past even infinitely remote. The delusion, however, faded rapidly as it came; and I mention it at all but to define the day of the last conversation I there held with my singular namesake.

The huge old house, with its countless subdivisions, had several large chambers communicating with each other, where slept the greater number of the students. There were, however (as must necessarily happen in a building so awkwardly planned), many little nooks or recesses, the odds and ends of the structure; and these the economic ingenuity of Dr Bransby had also fitted up as dormitories; although, being the merest closets, they were capable of accommodating but a single individual. One of these small apartments was occupied by Wilson.

One night, about the close of my fifth year at the school, and immediately after the altercation just mentioned, finding everyone wrapped in sleep, I arose from bed, and, lamp in hand, stole through a wilderness of narrow passages, from my own bedroom to that of my rival. I had long been plotting one of those ill-natured pieces of practical wit at his expense in which I had hitherto been so uniformly unsuccessful. It was my intention, now, to put my scheme in operation and I resolved to make him feel the whole extent of the malice with which I was imbued. Having reached his closet, I noiselessly entered, leaving the lamp, with a shade over it, on the outside. I advanced a step and listened to the sound of his tranquil breathing. Assured of his being asleep, I returned, took the light, and with it again approached the bed. Close curtains were around it, which, in the prosecution of my plan, I slowly and quietly withdrew, when the bright rays fell vividly upon the sleeper, and my eyes at the same moment, upon his countenance. I looked; and a numbness, an iciness of feeling instantly pervaded my frame. My breast heaved, my knees tottered, my whole spirit became possessed with an objectless yet intolerable horror. Gasping for breath, I lowered the lamp in still nearer proximity to the face. Were these – *these* the lineaments of William Wilson? I saw, indeed, that they were his, but I shook as if with a fit of the ague, in fancying they were not. What *was* there about them to confound me in this manner? I gazed; while my brain reeled with a multitude of incoherent thoughts. Not thus he appeared – assuredly not *thus* – in the vivacity of his waking hours. The same name! the same contour of person! the same day of arrival at the academy! And then his dogged and meaningless imitation of my gait, my voice, my habits, and my manner! Was it, in truth, within the bounds of human possibility, that *what I now saw* was the result, merely, of the habitual practice of this sarcastic imitation? Awe-stricken, and with a creeping shudder, I extinguished the lamp, passed silently from the chamber, and left, at once, the halls of that old academy, never to enter them again.

After a lapse of some months, spent at home in

mere idleness, I found myself a student at Eton. The brief interval had been sufficient to enfeeble my remembrance of the events at Dr Bransby's, or at least to effect a material change in the nature of the feelings with which I remembered them. The truth – the tragedy – of the drama was no more. I could now find room to doubt the evidence of my senses; and seldom called up the subject at all but with wonder at the extent of human credulity, and a smile at the vivid force of the imagination which I hereditarily possessed. Neither was this species of skepticism likely to be diminished by the character of the life I led at Eton. The vortex of thoughtless folly into which I there so immediately and so recklessly plunged, washed away all but the froth of my past hours, engulfed at once every solid or serious impression, and left to memory only the veriest levities of a former existence.

I do not wish, however, to trace the course of my miserable profligacy here – a profligacy which set at defiance the laws, while it eluded the vigilance of the institution. Three years of folly, passed without profit, had but given me rooted habits of vice, and added, in a somewhat unusual degree, to my bodily stature, when, after a week of soulless dissipation, I invited a small party of the most dissolute students to a secret carousal in my chambers. We met at a late hour of the night; for our debaucheries were to be faithfully protracted until morning. The wine flowed freely, and there were not wanting other and perhaps more dangerous seductions; so that the gray dawn had already faintly appeared in the east while our delirious extravagance was at its height. Madly flushed with cards and intoxication, I was in the act of insisting upon a toast of more than wonted profanity, when my attention was suddenly diverted by the violent, although partial, unclosing of the door of the apartment, and by the eager voice of a servant from without. He said that some person, apparently in great haste, demanded to speak with me in the hall.

Wildly excited with wine, the unexpected interruption rather delighted than surprised me. I staggered forward at once, and a few steps brought me to the vestibule of the building. In this low and small room there hung no lamp; and now no light at all was admitted, save that of the exceedingly feeble dawn which made its way through the semi-circular window. As I put my foot over the threshold, I became aware of the figure of a youth about my own height, and habited in a white kerseymere morning frock, cut in the novel fashion of the one I myself wore at the moment. This the faint light enabled me to perceive; but the features of his face I could not distinguish. Upon my entering, he strode hurriedly up to me, and, seizing me by the arm with a gesture of petulant impatience, whispered the words 'William Wilson' in my ear.

I grew perfectly sober in an instant.

There was that in the manner of the stranger, and in the tremulous shake of his uplifted finger, as he held it between my eyes and the light, which filled me with unqualified amazement; but it was not this which had so violently moved me. It was the pregnancy of solemn admonition in the singular, low, hissing utterance; and, above all, it was the character, the tone, *the key*, of those few, simple, and familiar, yet *whispered* syllables, which came with a thousand thronging memories of bygone days, and struck upon my soul with the shock of a galvanic battery. Ere I could recover the use of my senses he was gone.

Although this event failed not of a vivid effect upon my disordered imagination, yet was it evanescent as vivid. For some weeks, indeed, I busied myself in earnest inquiry, or was wrapped in a cloud of morbid speculation. I did not pretend to disguise from my perception the identity of the singular individual who thus perseveringly interfered with my affairs, and harassed me with his insinuated counsel. But who and what was this Wilson? – and whence came he? – and what were his purposes? Upon neither of these points could I be satisfied – merely ascertaining, in regard to him, that a sudden accident in his family had caused his removal from Dr Bransby's academy on the afternoon of the day in which I myself had eloped. But in a brief period I ceased to think upon the subject, my attention being all absorbed in a contemplated departure for Oxford. Thither

I soon went, the uncalculating vanity of my parents furnishing me with an outfit and annual establishment, which would enable me to indulge at will in the luxury already so dear to my heart – to vie in profuseness of expenditure with the haughtiest heirs of the wealthiest earldoms in Great Britain.

Excited by such appliances to vice, my constitutional temperament broke forth with redoubled ardor, and I spurned even the common restraints of decency in the mad infatuation of my revels. But it were absurd to pause in the detail of my extravagance. Let it suffice, that among spendthrifts I out-Heroded Herod, and that, giving name to a multitude of novel follies, I added no brief appendix to the long catalogue of vices then usual in the most dissolute university of Europe.

It could hardly be credited, however, that I had, even here, so utterly fallen from the gentlemanly estate, as to seek acquaintance with the vilest arts of the gambler by profession, and, having become an adept in his despicable science, to practice it habitually as a means of increasing my already enormous income at the expense of the weak-minded among my fellow-colleagians. Such, nevertheless, was the fact. And the very enormity of this offence against all manly and honorable sentiment proved, beyond doubt, the main if not the sole reason of the impunity with which it was committed. Who, indeed, among my most abandoned associates, would not rather have disputed the clearest evidence of his senses, than have suspected of such courses, the gay, the frank, the generous William Wilson – the noblest and most liberal commoner at Oxford – him whose follies (said his parasites) were but the follies of youth and unbridled fancy – whose errors but inimitable whim – whose darkest vice but a careless and dashing extravagance?

I had been now two years successfully busied in this way, when there came to the university a young *parvenu* nobleman, Glendinning – rich, said report, as Herodes Atticus – his riches, too, as easily acquired. I soon found him of weak intellect, and, of course, marked him as a fitting subject for my skill. I frequently engaged him in play, and contrived, with the gambler's usual art, to let him win considerable sums, the more effectually to entangle him in my snares. At length, my schemes being ripe, I met him (with the full intention that this meeting should be final and decisive) at the chambers of a fellow-commoner (Mr Preston), equally intimate with both, but who, to do him justice, entertained not even a remote suspicion of my design. To give to this a better coloring, I had contrived to have assembled a party of some eight or ten, and was solicitously careful that the introduction of cards should appear accidental, and originate in the proposal of my contemplated dupe himself. To be brief upon a vile topic, none of the low finesse was omitted, so customary upon similar occasions, that it is a just matter for wonder

how any are still found so besotted as to fall its
victim.

We had protracted our sitting far into the night,
and I had at length effected the manoeuvre of
getting Glendinning as my sole antagonist. The
game, too, was my favorite *écarté*. The rest of the
company, interested in the extent of our play, had
abandoned their own cards, and were standing
around us as spectators. The *parvenu*, who had
been induced by my artifices in the early part of
the evening, to drink deeply, now shuffled, dealt,
or played, with a wild nervousness of manner for
which his intoxication, I thought, might partially,
but could not altogether account. In a very short
period he had become my debtor to a large
amount, when, having taken a long draught of
port, he did precisely what I had been coolly
anticipating – he proposed to double our already
extravagant stakes. With a well-feigned show of
reluctance, and not until after my repeated refusal
had seduced him into some angry words which
gave a color of *pique* to my compliance, did I
finally comply. The result, of course, did but
prove how entirely the prey was in my toils: in
less than an hour he had quadrupled his debt. For
some time his countenance had been losing the
florid tinge lent it by the wine; but now, to my
astonishment, I perceived that it had grown to a
pallor truly fearful. I say, to my astonishment.
Glendinning had been represented to my eager
inquiries as immeasurably wealthy; and the sums

which he had as yet lost, although in themselves vast, could not, I supposed, very seriously annoy, much less so violently affect him. That he was overcome by the wine just swallowed, was the idea which most readily presented itself; and, rather with a view to the preservation of my own character in the eyes of my associates, than from any less interested motive, I was about to insist, peremptorily, upon a discontinuance of the play, when some expressions at my elbow from among the company, and an ejaculation evincing utter despair on the part of Glendinning, gave me to understand that I had effected his total ruin under circumstances which, rendering him an object for the pity of all, should have protected him from the ill offices even of a fiend.

What now might have been my conduct it is difficult to say. The pitiable condition of my dupe had thrown an air of embarrassed gloom over all; and, for some moments, a profound silence was maintained, during which I could not help feeling my cheeks tingle with the many burning glances of scorn or reproach cast upon me by the less abandoned of the party. I will even own that an intolerable weight of anxiety was for a brief instant lifted from my bosom by the sudden and extra-ordinary interruption which ensued. The wide, heavy folding doors of the apartment were all at once thrown open, to their full extent, with a vigorous and rushing impetuosity that extin-guished, as if by magic, every candle in the room.

Their light, in dying, enabled us just to perceive that a stranger had entered, about my own height, and closely muffled in a cloak. The darkness, however, was not total; and we could only *feel* that he was standing in our midst. Before any one of us could recover from the extreme astonishment into which this rudeness had thrown all, we heard the voice of the intruder.

'Gentlemen,' he said, in a low, distinct, and never-to-be-forgotten *whisper* which thrilled to the very marrow of my bones, 'Gentlemen, I make no apology for this behavior, because in thus behaving, I am fulfilling a duty. You are, beyond doubt, uninformed of the true character of the person who has tonight won at *écarté* a large sum of money from Lord Glendinning. I will therefore put you upon an expeditious and decisive plan of obtaining this very necessary information. Please to examine, at your leisure, the inner linings of the cuff of his left sleeve, and the several little packages which may be found in the somewhat capacious pockets of his embroidered morning wrapper.'

While he spoke, so profound was the stillness that one might have heard a pin drop upon the floor. In ceasing, he departed at once, and as abruptly as he had entered. Can I – shall I describe my sensations? Must I say that I felt all the horrors of the damned? Most assuredly I had little time for reflection. Many hands roughly seized me upon the spot, and lights were immediately reprocured. A search ensued. In the lining of my sleeve were found all the court cards essential in _écarté_, and, in the pockets of my wrapper, a number of packs, facsimiles of those used at our sittings, with the single exception that mine were of the species called, technically, _arrondées_; the honors being slightly convex at the ends, the lower cards slightly convex at the sides. In this disposition, the dupe who cuts, as customary, at the length of the pack, will invariably find that he cuts his antagonist an honor; while the gambler, cutting at the breadth, will, as certainly, cut nothing for his victim which may count in the records of the game.

Any burst of indignation upon this discovery would have affected me less than the silent contempt, or the sarcastic composure, with which it was received.

'Mr Wilson,' said our host, stooping to remove from beneath his feet an exceedingly luxurious cloak of rare furs, 'Mr Wilson, this is your property.' (The weather was cold; and, upon quitting my own room, I had thrown a cloak over my dressing wrapper, putting it off upon reaching the scene of play.) 'I presume it is supererogatory to seek here (eyeing the folds of the garment with a bitter smile) for any farther evidence of your skill. Indeed, we have had enough. You will see the necessity, I hope, of quitting Oxford – at all events, of quitting instantly my chambers.'

Abased, humbled to the dust as I then was, it is

probable that I should have resented this galling language by immediate personal violence, had not my whole attention been at the moment arrested by a fact of the most startling character. The cloak which I had worn was of a rare description of fur; how rare, how extravagantly costly, I shall not venture to say. Its fashion, too, was of my own fantastic invention; for I was fastidious to an absurd degree of coxcombry, in matters of this frivolous nature. When, therefore, Mr Preston reached me that which he had picked up upon the floor, and near the folding-doors of the apartment, it was with an astonishment nearly bordering upon terror, that I perceived my own already hanging on my arm (where I had no doubt unwittingly placed it), and that the one presented me was but its exact counterpart in every, in even the minutest possible particular. The singular being who had so disastrously exposed me, had been muffled, I remembered, in a cloak; and none had been worn at all by any of the members of our party, with the exception of myself. Retaining some presence of mind, I took the one offered me by Preston; placed it, unnoticed, over my own; left the apartment with a resolute scowl of defiance; and, next morning ere dawn of day, commenced a hurried journey from Oxford to the continent, in a perfect agony of horror and of shame.

I fled in vain. My evil destiny pursued me as if in exultation, and proved, indeed, that the exercise of its mysterious dominion had as yet only begun. Scarcely had I set foot in Paris, ere I had fresh evidence of the detestable interest taken by this Wilson in my concerns. Years flew, while I experienced no relief. Villain! – at Rome, with how untimely, yet with how spectral an officiousness, stepped he in between me and my ambition! at Vienna, too – at Berlin – and at Moscow! Where, in truth, had I *not* bitter cause to curse him within my heart? From his inscrutable tyranny did I at length flee, panic-stricken, as from a pestilence; and to the very ends of the earth *I fled in vain*.

And again, and again, in secret communion with my own spirit, would I demand the questions 'Who is he? – whence came he? – and what are his objects?' But no answer was there found. And now I scrutinized, with a minute scrutiny, the forms, and the methods, and the leading traits of his impertinent supervision. But even here there was very little upon which to base a conjecture. It was noticeable, indeed, that, in no one of the multiplied instances in which he had of late crossed my path, had he so crossed it except to frustrate those schemes, or to disturb those actions, which, if fully carried out, might have resulted in bitter mischief. Poor justification this, in truth, for an authority so imperiously assumed! Poor indemnity for natural rights of self-agency so pertinaciously, so insultingly denied!

I had also been forced to notice that my tormentor, for a very long period of time (while

scrupulously and with miraculous dexterity maintaining his whim of an identity of apparel with
myself) had so contrived it, in the execution of his
varied interference with my will, that I saw not, at
any moment, the features of his face. Be Wilson
what he might, *this*, at least, was but the veriest of
affectation, or of folly. Could he, for an instant,
have supposed that, in my admonisher at Eton –
in the destroyer of my honor at Oxford – in him
who thwarted my ambition at Rome, my revenge
at Paris, my passionate love at Naples, or what he
falsely termed my avarice in Egypt – that in this,
my arch-enemy and evil genius, I could fail to
recognize the William Wilson of my school-boy
days – the namesake, the companion, the rival –
the hated and dreaded rival at Dr Bransby's?
Impossible! – But let me hasten to the last eventful
scene of the drama.

Thus far I had succumbed supinely to this
imperious domination. The sentiment of deep awe
with which I habitually regarded the elevated
character, the majestic wisdom, the apparent omni-
presence and omnipotence of Wilson, added to a
feeling of even terror, with which certain other
traits in his nature and assumptions inspired me,
had operated, hitherto, to impress me with an idea
of my own utter weakness and helplessness, and to
suggest an implicit, although bitterly reluctant
submission to his arbitrary will. But, of late days,
I had given myself up entirely to wine; and its
maddening influence upon my hereditary temper

rendered me more and more impatient of control. I began to murmur – to hesitate – to resist. And was it only fancy which induced me to believe that, with the increase of my own firmness, that of my tormentor underwent a proportional diminution? Be this as it may, I now began to feel the inspiration of a burning hope, and at length nurtured in my secret thoughts a stern and desperate resolution that I would submit no longer to be enslaved.

It was at Rome, during the Carnival of 18—, that I attended a masquerade in the palazzo of the Neapolitan Duke Di Broglio. I had indulged more freely than usual in the excesses of the wine-table; and now the suffocating atmosphere of the crowded rooms irritated me beyond endurance. The difficulty, too, of forcing my way through the mazes of the company contributed not a little to the ruffling of my temper; for I was anxiously seeking (let me not say with what unworthy motive) the young, the gay, the beautiful wife of the aged and doting Di Broglio. With a too unscrupulous confidence she had previously communicated to me the secret of the costume in which she would be habited, and now, having caught a glimpse of her person, I was hurrying to make my way into her presence. At this moment I felt a light hand placed upon my shoulder, and that ever-remembered, low, damnable *whisper* within my ear.

In an absolute frenzy of wrath, I turned at once

upon him who had thus interrupted me, and seized him violently by the collar. He was attired, as I had expected, in a costume altogether similar to my own; wearing a Spanish cloak of blue velvet, begirt about the waist with a crimson belt sustaining a rapier. A mask of black silk entirely covered his face.

'Scoundrel!' I said, in a voice husky with rage, while every syllable I uttered seemed as new fuel to my fury; 'scoundrel! impostor! accursed villain! you shall not – you *shall not* dog me unto death! Follow me, or I stab you where you stand!' – and I broke my way from the ballroom into a small antechamber adjoining, dragging him unresistingly with me as I went.

Upon entering, I thrust him furiously from me. He staggered against the wall, while I closed the door with an oath, and commanded him to draw. He hesitated but for an instant; then, with a slight sigh, drew in silence, and put himself upon his defence.

The contest was brief indeed. I was frantic with every species of wild excitement, and felt within my single arm the energy and power of a multitude. In a few seconds I forced him by sheer strength against the wainscotting, and thus, getting him at mercy, plunged my sword, with brute ferocity, repeatedly through and through his bosom.

At that instant some person tried the latch of the door. I hastened to prevent an intrusion, and

then immediately returned to my dying antagonist. But what human language can adequately
portray *that* astonishment, *that* horror which possessed me at the spectacle then presented to view?
The brief moment in which I averted my eyes had
been sufficient to produce, apparently, a material
change in the arrangements at the upper or farther
end of the room. A large mirror – so at first it
seemed to me in my confusion – now stood where
none had been perceptible before; and as I stepped
up to it in extremity of terror, mine own image,
but with features all pale and dabbled in blood,
advanced to meet me with a feeble and tottering
gait.

Thus it appeared, I say, but was not. It was my
antagonist – it was Wilson, who then stood before
me in the agonies of his dissolution. His mask and
cloak lay, where he had thrown them, upon the
floor. Not a thread in all his raiment – not a line
in all the marked and singular lineaments of his
face which was not, even in the most absolute
identity, *mine own*!

It was Wilson; but he spoke no longer in a
whisper, and I could have fancied that I myself
was speaking while he said:

'*You have conquered, and I yield. Yet hencefor-
ward art thou also dead – dead to the World, to
Heaven, and to Hope! In me didst thou exist – and,
in my death, see by this image, which is thine own,
how utterly thou hast murdered thyself.*'

THE BLACK CAT

For the most wild yet most homely narrative which I am about to pen, I neither expect nor solicit belief. Mad indeed would I be to expect it, in a case where my very senses reject their own evidence. Yet, mad am I not – and very surely do I not dream. But tomorrow I die, and today I would unburden my soul. My immediate purpose is to place before the world, plainly, succinctly, and without comment, a series of mere household events. In their consequences, these events have terrified – have tortured – have destroyed me. Yet I will not attempt to expound them. To me, they have presented little but horror – to many they will seem less terrible than *baroques*. Hereafter, perhaps, some intellect may be found which will reduce my phantasm to the commonplace – some intellect more calm, more logical, and far less excitable than my own, which will perceive, in the circumstances I detail with awe, nothing more than an ordinary succession of very natural causes and effects.

From my infancy I was noted for the docility and humanity of my disposition. My tenderness of heart was even so conspicuous as to make me the jest of my companions. I was especially fond of animals, and was indulged by my parents with a great variety of pets. With these I spent most of my time, and never was so happy as when feeding and caressing them. This peculiarity of character grew with my growth, and, in my manhood, I derived from it one of my principal sources of pleasure. To those who have cherished an affection for a faithful and sagacious dog, I need hardly be at the trouble of explaining the nature or the intensity of the gratification thus derivable. There is something in the unselfish and self-sacrificing love of a brute, which goes directly to the heart of him who has had frequent occasion to test the paltry friendship and gossamer fidelity of mere *Man*.

I married early, and was happy to find in my wife a disposition not uncongenial with my own. Observing my partiality for domestic pets, she lost no opportunity of procuring those of the most agreeable kind. We had birds, goldfish, a fine dog, rabbits, a small monkey, and a *cat*.

This latter was a remarkably large and beautiful animal, entirely black, and sagacious to an astonishing degree. In speaking of his intelligence, my wife, who at heart was not a little tinctured with superstition, made frequent allusion to the ancient popular notion, which regarded all black cats as witches in disguise. Not that she was ever *serious* upon this point – and I mention the matter at all for no better reason than that it happens, just now, to be remembered.

Pluto – this was the cat's name – was my favorite pet and playmate. I alone fed him, and he attended me wherever I went about the house. It was even with difficulty that I could prevent him from following me through the streets.

Our friendship lasted, in this manner, for several years, during which my general temperament and character – through the instrumentality of the Fiend Intemperance – had (I blush to confess it) experienced a radical alteration for the worse. I grew, day by day, more moody, more irritable, more regardless of the feelings of others. I suffered myself to use intemperate language to my wife. At length, I even offered her personal violence. My pets, of course, were made to feel the change in my disposition. I not only neglected, but ill-used them. For Pluto, however, I still retained sufficient regard to restrain me from maltreating him, as I made no scruple of maltreating the rabbits, the monkey, or even the dog, when, by accident, or through affection, they came in my way. But my disease grew upon me – for what disease is like Alcohol! – and at length even Pluto, who was now becoming old, and consequently somewhat peevish – even Pluto began to experience the effects of my ill temper.

One night, returning home, much intoxicated, from one of my haunts about town, I fancied that the cat avoided my presence. I seized him; when, in his fright at my violence, he inflicted a slight wound upon my hand with his teeth. The fury of a demon instantly possessed me. I knew myself no longer. My original soul seemed, at once, to take its flight from my body; and a more than fiendish malevolence, gin-nurtured, thrilled every fibre of my frame. I took from my waistcoat-pocket a penknife, opened it, grasped the poor beast by the throat, and deliberately cut one of its eyes from the socket! I blush, I burn, I shudder, while I pen the damnable atrocity.

When reason returned with the morning – when I had slept off the fumes of the night's debauch – I experienced a sentiment half of horror, half of remorse, from the crime of which I had been guilty; but it was, at best, a feeble and equivocal feeling, and the soul remained untouched. I again plunged into excess, and soon drowned in wine all memory of the deed.

In the mean time the cat slowly recovered. The socket of the lost eye presented, it is true, a frightful appearance, but he no longer appeared to suffer any pain. He went about the house as usual, but, as might be expected, fled in extreme terror at my approach. I had so much of my old heart left, as to be at first grieved by this evident dislike on the part of a creature which had once so loved me. But this feeling soon gave place to irritation. And then came, as if to my final and irrevocable overthrow, the spirit of PERVERSENESS. Of this spirit philosophy takes no account. Yet I am not more sure that my soul lives, than I am that perverseness is one of the primitive impulses of the human heart – one of the indivisible primary faculties, or sentiments, which give direction to the character of Man. Who has not, a hundred times, found himself committing a vile or a stupid action, for no other reason than because he knows he should *not*? Have we not a perpetual inclination, in the teeth of our best judgment, to violate that which is *Law*, merely because we understand it to be such? This spirit of perverseness, I say, came to my final overthrow. It was this unfathomable longing of the soul *to vex itself* – to offer violence to its own nature – to do wrong for the wrong's sake only – that urged me to continue and finally to consummate the injury I had inflicted upon the unoffending brute. One morning, in cold blood, I slipped a noose about its neck and hung it to the limb of a tree; hung it with the tears streaming from my eyes, and with the bitterest remorse at my heart; hung it *because* I knew that it had loved me, and *because* I felt it had given me no reason of offence; hung it *because* I knew that in so doing I was committing a sin – a deadly sin that would so jeopardize my immortal soul as to place it – if such a thing were possible – even beyond the reach of the infinite mercy of the Most Merciful and Most Terrible God.

On the night of the day on which this most cruel deed was done, I was aroused from sleep by the cry of fire. The curtains of my bed were in flames. The whole house was blazing. It was with great difficulty that my wife, a servant, and myself, made our escape from the conflagration. The destruction was complete. My entire worldly wealth was swallowed up, and I resigned myself thenceforward to despair.

I am above the weakness of seeking to establish a sequence of cause and effect, between the disaster and the atrocity. But I am detailing a chain of facts – and wish not to leave even a possible link imperfect. On the day succeeding the fire, I visited the ruins. The walls, with one exception, had fallen in. This exception was found in a compartment wall, not very thick, which stood about the middle of the house, and against which had rested the head of my bed. The plastering had here, in great measure, resisted the action of the fire – a fact which I attributed to its having been recently spread. About this wall a dense crowd were collected, and many persons seemed to be examining a particular portion of it with very minute and eager attention. The words 'strange!' 'singular!' and other similar expressions, excited my curiosity. I approached and saw, as if graven in *bas-relief* upon the white surface, the figure of a gigantic *cat*. The impression was given with an accuracy truly marvellous. There was a rope about the animal's neck.

When I first beheld this apparition – for I could scarcely regard it as less – my wonder and my terror were extreme. But at length reflection came to my aid. The cat, I remembered, had been hung in a garden adjacent to the house. Upon the alarm of fire, this garden had been immediately filled by the crowd – by some one of whom the animal must have been cut from the tree and thrown, through an open window, into my chamber. This had probably been done with the view of arousing me from sleep. The falling of other walls had compressed the victim of my cruelty into the substance of the freshly spread plaster; the lime of which, with the flames, and the *ammonia* from the carcass, had then accomplished the portraiture as I saw it.

Although I thus readily accounted to my reason, if not altogether to my conscience, for the startling fact just detailed, it did not the less fail to make a deep impression upon my fancy. For months I could not rid myself of the phantasm of the cat; and, during this period, there came back into my spirit a half-sentiment that seemed, but was not, remorse. I went so far as to regret the loss of the animal, and to look about me, among the vile haunts which I now habitually frequented, for another pet of the same species, and of somewhat similar appearance, with which to supply its place.

One night as I sat, half stupefied, in a den of more than infamy, my attention was suddenly drawn to some black object, reposing upon the head of one of the immense hogsheads of gin, or of rum, which constituted the chief furniture of the apartment. I had been looking steadily at the top of this hogshead for some minutes, and what now caused me surprise was the fact that I had not sooner perceived the object thereupon. I approached it, and touched it with my hand. It was a black cat – a very large one – fully as large as Pluto, and closely resembling him in every respect but one. Pluto had not a white hair upon any portion of his body; but this cat had a large, although indefinite splotch of white, covering nearly the whole region of the breast.

Upon my touching him, he immediately arose, purred loudly, rubbed against my hand, and appeared delighted with my notice. This, then, was the very creature of which I was in search. I at once offered to purchase it of the landlord; but this person made no claim to it – knew nothing of it – had never seen it before.

I continued my caresses, and when I prepared to go home, the animal evinced a disposition to accompany me. I permitted it to do so; occasionally stooping and patting it as I proceeded. When it reached the house it domesticated itself at once, and became immediately a great favorite with my wife.

For my own part, I soon found a dislike to it arising within me. This was just the reverse of what I had anticipated; but – I know not how or why it was – its evident fondness for myself rather disgusted and annoyed me. By slow degrees these feelings of disgust and annoyance rose into the bitterness of hatred. I avoided the creature; a certain sense of shame, and the remembrance of my former deed of cruelty, preventing me from physically abusing it. I did not, for some weeks, strike, or otherwise violently ill use it; but gradually – very gradually – I came to look upon it with unutterable loathing, and to flee silently from its odious presence, as from the breath of a pestilence.

What added, no doubt, to my hatred of the beast, was the discovery, on the morning after I brought it home, that, like Pluto, it also had been deprived of one of its eyes. This circumstance, however, only endeared it to my wife, who, as I have already said, possessed, in a high degree, that humanity of feeling which had once been my distinguishing trait, and the source of many of my simplest and purest pleasures.

With my aversion to this cat, however, its partiality for myself seemed to increase. It followed my footsteps with a pertinacity which it would be difficult to make the reader comprehend. Whenever I sat, it would crouch beneath my chair, or spring upon my knees, covering me with its loathsome caresses. If I arose to walk it would get between my feet and thus nearly throw me down, or, fastening its long and sharp claws in my dress, clamber, in this manner, to my breast. At such times, although I longed to destroy it with a blow, I was yet withheld from so doing, partly by a memory of my former crime, but chiefly – let me confess it at once – by absolute *dread* of the beast.

This dread was not exactly a dread of physical evil – and yet I should be at a loss how otherwise to define it. I am almost ashamed to own – yes, even in this felon's cell, I am almost ashamed to own – that the terror and horror with which the animal inspired me, had been heightened by one of the merest chimeras it would be possible to conceive. My wife had called my attention, more than once, to the character of the mark of white hair, of which I have spoken, and which consti- tuted the sole visible difference between the strange beast and the one I had destroyed. The reader will remember that this mark, although large, had been originally very indefinite; but, by slow degrees – degrees nearly imperceptible, and which for a long time my reason struggled to reject as fanciful – it had, at length, assumed a rigorous distinctness of outline. It was now the representation of an object that I shudder to name – and for this, above all, I loathed, and dreaded, and would have rid myself of the monster *had I dared* – it was now, I say, the image of a hideous – of a ghastly thing – of the GALLOWS! – oh, mourn- ful and terrible engine of Horror and of Crime – of Agony and of Death!

And now was I indeed wretched beyond the wretchedness of mere Humanity. And *a brute beast* – whose fellow I had contemptuously destroyed – *a brute beast* to work out for *me* – for me, a man fashioned in the image of the High God – so much of insufferable woe! Alas! neither by day nor by night knew I the blessing of rest any more! During the former the creature left me no moment alone, and in the latter I started hourly from dreams of unutterable fear to find the hot breath of *the thing* upon my face, and its vast weight – an incarnate nightmare that I had no power to shake off – incumbent eternally upon my *heart*!

Beneath the pressure of torments such as these the feeble remnant of the good within me succumbed. Evil thoughts became my sole intimates – the darkest and most evil of thoughts. The moodiness of my usual temper increased to hatred of all things and of all mankind; while from the sudden, frequent, and ungovernable outbursts of a fury to which I now blindly abandoned myself, my uncomplaining wife, alas, was the most usual and the most patient of sufferers.

One day she accompanied me, upon some household errand, into the cellar of the old building which our poverty compelled us to inhabit. The cat followed me down the steep stairs, and, nearly throwing me headlong, exasperated me to madness. Uplifting an axe, and forgetting in my wrath the childish dread which had hitherto stayed my hand, I aimed a blow at the animal, which, of course, would have proved instantly fatal had it descended as I wished. But this blow was arrested by the hand of my wife. Goaded by the interference into a rage more than demoniacal, I withdrew my arm from her grasp and buried the axe in her brain. She fell dead upon the spot without a groan.

This hideous murder accomplished, I set myself forthwith, and with entire deliberation, to the task of concealing the body. I knew that I could not remove it from the house, either by day or by night, without the risk of being observed by the neighbors. Many projects entered my mind. At one period I thought of cutting the corpse into minute fragments, and destroying them by fire. At another, I resolved to dig a grave for it in the floor of the cellar. Again, I deliberated about casting it in the well in the yard – about packing it in a box, as if merchandise, with the usual arrangements, and so getting a porter to take it from the house. Finally I hit upon what I considered a far better expedient than either of these. I determined to wall it up in the cellar, as the monks of the Middle Ages are recorded to have walled up their victims.

For a purpose such as this the cellar was well adapted. Its walls were loosely constructed, and had lately been plastered throughout with a rough plaster, which the dampness of the atmosphere had prevented from hardening. Moreover, in one of the walls was a projection, caused by a false chimney, or fireplace, that had been filled up and made to resemble the rest of the cellar. I made no doubt that I could readily displace the bricks at this point, insert the corpse, and wall the whole up as before, so that no eye could detect anything suspicious.

And in this calculation I was not deceived. By means of a crowbar I easily dislodged the bricks, and, having carefully deposited the body against the inner wall, I propped it in that position, while with little trouble I relaid the whole structure as it originally stood. Having procured mortar, sand, and hair, with every possible precaution, I prepared a plaster which could not be distinguished from the old, and with this I very carefully went over the new brick-work. When I had finished, I felt satisfied that all was right. The wall did not present the slightest appearance of having been disturbed. The rubbish on the floor was picked up with the minutest care. I looked around triumphantly, and said to myself: 'Here at least, then, my labor has not been in vain.'

My next step was to look for the beast which had been the cause of so much wretchedness; for I had, at length, firmly resolved to put it to death. Had I been able to meet with it at the moment, there could have been no doubt of its fate; but it appeared that the crafty animal had been alarmed at the violence of my previous anger, and forbore to present itself in my present mood. It is impossible to describe or to imagine the deep, the blissful sense of relief which the absence of the detested creature occasioned in my bosom. It did not make its appearance during the night; and thus for one night, at least, since its introduction into the house, I soundly and tranquilly slept; aye, *slept* even with the burden of murder upon my soul.

The second and the third day passed, and still my tormentor came not. Once again I breathed as a freeman. The monster, in terror, had fled the premises for ever! I should behold it no more! My happiness was supreme! The guilt of my dark deed disturbed me but little. Some few inquiries had been made, but these had been readily answered. Even a search had been instituted – but of course nothing was to be discovered. I looked upon my future felicity as secured.

Upon the fourth day of the assassination, a party of the police came, very unexpectedly, into the house, and proceeded again to make rigorous investigation of the premises. Secure, however, in the inscrutability of my place of concealment, I felt no embarrassment whatever. The officers bade me accompany them in their search. They left no nook or corner unexplored. At length, for the third or fourth time, they descended into the cellar. I quivered not in a muscle. My heart beat calmly as that of one who slumbers in innocence. I walked the cellar from end to end. I folded my arms upon my bosom, and roamed easily to and fro. The police were thoroughly satisfied and prepared to depart. The glee at my heart was too strong to be restrained. I burned to say if but one word, by way of triumph, and to render doubly sure their assurance of my guiltlessness.

'Gentlemen,' I said at last, as the party ascended the steps, 'I delight to have allayed your suspicions. I wish you all health and a little more courtesy. By the bye, gentlemen, this – this is a very well-constructed house,' (in the rabid desire to say something easily, I scarcely knew what I uttered at all) – 'I may say an *excellently* well-constructed house. These walls – you are going, gentlemen? – these walls are solidly put together'; and here, through the mere frenzy of bravado, I rapped heavily with a cane which I held in my hand, upon that very portion of the brickwork behind which stood the corpse of the wife of my bosom.

But may God shield and deliver me from the fangs of the Arch-Fiend! No sooner had the reverberation of my blows sunk into silence, than I was answered by a voice from within the tomb! – by a cry, at first muffled and broken, like the sobbing of a child, and then quickly swelling into one long, loud, and continuous scream, utterly anomalous and inhuman – a howl – a wailing shriek, half of horror and half of triumph, such as might have arisen only out of hell, conjointly from the throats of the damned in their agony and of the demons that exult in the damnation.

Of my own thoughts it is folly to speak. Swooning, I staggered to the opposite wall. For one instant the party on the stairs remained motionless, through extremity of terror and awe. In the next a dozen stout arms were toiling at the wall. It fell bodily. The corpse, already greatly decayed and clotted with gore, stood erect before the eyes of the spectators. Upon its head, with red extended mouth and solitary eye of fire, sat the hideous beast whose craft had seduced me into murder, and whose informing voice had consigned me to the hangman. I had walled the monster up within the tomb.

The Pit and the Pendulum

Inpia tortorum longas hic turba furores
Sanguinis innocui, non satiata, aluit.
Sospite nunc patria, fracto nunc funeris antro,
Mors ubi dira fuit vita salusque patent.
[*Quatrain composed for the gates of a market to be erected upon the site of the Jacobin Club House at Paris*.]

I was sick – sick unto death with that long agony; and when they at length unbound me, and I was permitted to sit, I felt that my senses were leaving me. The sentence – the dread sentence of death – was the last of distinct accentuation which reached my ears. After that, the sound of the inquisitorial voices seemed merged in one dreamy indeterminate hum. It conveyed to my soul the idea of *revolution* – perhaps from its association, in fancy with the burr of a mill-wheel. This only for a brief period, for presently I heard no more. Yet, for a while, I saw – but with how terrible an exaggeration! I saw the lips of the black-robed judges. They appeared to me white – whiter than the sheet upon which I trace these words – and thin even to grotesqueness; thin with the intensity of their expression of firmness – of immovable resolution – of stern contempt of human torture. I saw that the decrees of what to me was Fate were still issuing from those lips. I saw them writhe with a deadly locution. I saw them fashion the syllables of my name; and I shuddered because no sound succeeded. I saw, too, for a few moments of delirious horror, the soft and nearly imperceptible waving of the sable draperies which enwrapped the walls of the apartment. And then my vision fell upon the seven tall candles upon the table. At first they wore the aspect of charity, and seemed white slender angels who would save me; but then, all at once, there came a most deadly nausea over my spirit, and I felt every fibre in my frame thrill as if I had touched the wire of a galvanic battery, while the angel forms became meaningless spectres, with heads of flame, and I saw that from them there would be no help. And then there stole into my fancy, like a rich musical note, the thought of what sweet rest there must be in the grave. The thought came gently and stealthily, and it seemed long before it attained full appreciation; but just as my spirit came at length properly to feel and entertain it, the figures of the judges vanished, as if magically, from before me; the tall candles sank into nothingness; their flames went out utterly; the blackness of darkness supervened; all sensations appeared swallowed up in a mad rushing descent as of the soul into Hades.

Then silence, and stillness, and night were the universe.

I had swooned; but still will not say that all of consciousness was lost. What of it there remained I will not attempt to define, or even to describe; yet all was not lost. In the deepest slumber – no! In delirium – no! In a swoon – no! In death – no! even in the grave all *is not* lost. Else there is no immortality for man. Arousing from the most profound of slumbers, we break the gossamer web of *some* dream. Yet in a second afterward (so frail may that web have been) we remember not that we have dreamed. In the return to life from the swoon there are two stages: first, that of the sense of mental or spiritual; secondly, that of the sense of physical, existence. It seems probable that if, upon reaching the second stage, we could recall the impressions of the first, we should find these impressions eloquent in memories of the gulf beyond. And that gulf is – what? How at least shall we distinguish its shadows from those of the tomb? But if the impressions of what I have termed the first stage are not, at will, recalled, yet, after long interval, do they not come unbidden, while we marvel whence they come? He who has never swooned, is not he who finds strange palaces and wildly familiar faces in coals that glow; is not he who beholds floating in mid-air the sad visions that the many may not view; is not he who ponders over the perfume of some novel flower; is not he whose brain grows bewildered with the meaning of some musical cadence which has never before arrested his attention.

Amid frequent and thoughtful endeavors to remember, amid earnest struggles to regather some token of the state of seeming nothingness into which my soul had lapsed, there have been moments when I have dreamed of success; there have been brief, very brief periods when I have conjured up remembrances which the lucid reason of a later epoch assures me could have had reference only to that condition of seeming unconsciousness. These shadows of memory tell, indistinctly, of tall figures that lifted and bore me in silence down – down – still down – till a hideous dizziness oppressed me at the mere idea of the interminableness of the descent. They tell also of a vague horror at my heart, on account of that heart's unnatural stillness. Then comes a sense of sudden motionlessness throughout all things; as if those who bore me (a ghastly train!) had outrun, in their descent, the limits of the limitless, and paused from the wearisomeness of their toil. After this I call to mind flatness and dampness; and then all is *madness* – the madness of a memory which busies itself among forbidden things.

Very suddenly there came back to my soul motion and sound – the tumultuous motion of the heart, and, in my ears, the sound of its beating. Then a pause in which all is blank. Then again sound, and motion, and touch – a tingling sensation pervading my frame. Then the mere consciousness of existence, without thought – a condition which lasted long. Then, very suddenly, *thought*, and shuddering terror, and earnest endeavor to comprehend my true state. Then a strong desire to lapse into insensibility. Then a rushing revival of soul and a successful effort to move. And now a full memory of the trial, of the judges, of the sable draperies, of the sentence, of the sickness, of the swoon. Then entire forgetfulness of all that followed; of all that a later day and much earnestness of endeavor have enabled me vaguely to recall.

So far, I had not opened my eyes. I felt that I lay upon my back, unbound. I reached out my hand, and it fell heavily upon something damp and hard. There I suffered it to remain for many minutes, while I strove to imagine where and *what* I could be. I longed, yet dared not, to employ my vision. I dreaded the first glance at objects around me. It was not that I feared to look upon things horrible, but that I grew aghast lest there should be *nothing* to see. At length, with a wild desperation at heart, I quickly unclosed my eyes. My worst thoughts, then, were confirmed. The blackness of eternal night encompassed me. I struggled for breath. The intensity of the darkness seemed to oppress and stifle me. The atmosphere was intolerably close. I still lay quietly, and made effort to exercise my reason. I brought to mind the inquisitorial proceedings, and attempted from that point to deduce my real condition. The sentence had passed; and it appeared to me that a very long interval of time had since elapsed. Yet not for a moment did I suppose myself actually dead. Such a supposition, notwithstanding what we read in fiction, is altogether inconsistent with real existence; but where and in what state was I? The condemned to death, I knew, perished usually at the *autos-da-fé*, and one of these had been held on the very night of the day of my trial. Had I been remanded to my dungeon, to await the next sacrifice, which would not take place for many months? This I at once saw could not be. Victims had been in immediate demand. Moreover, my dungeon, as well as all the condemned cells at Toledo, had stone floors, and light was not altogether excluded.

A fearful idea now suddenly drove the blood in torrents upon my heart, and for a brief period I once more relapsed into insensibility. Upon recovering, I at once started to my feet, trembling convulsively in every fibre. I thrust my arms wildly above and around me in all directions. I felt nothing; yet dreaded to move a step, lest I should be impeded by the walls of a *tomb*. Perspiration burst from every pore, and stood in cold big beads upon my forehead. The agony of suspense grew at length intolerable, and I cautiously moved forward, with my arms extended, and my eyes straining from their sockets in the hope of catching some faint ray of light. I proceeded for many paces; but still all was blackness and vacancy. I breathed more freely. It seemed evident that mine was not, at least, the most hideous of fates.

And now, as I still continued to step cautiously onward, there came thronging upon my recollection a thousand vague rumors of the horrors of Toledo. Of the dungeons there had been strange things narrated – fables I had always deemed them – but yet strange, and too ghastly to repeat, save in a whisper. Was I left to perish of starvation in this subterranean world of darkness; or what fate, perhaps even more fearful, awaited me? That the result would be death, and a death of more than customary bitterness, I knew too well the character of my judges to doubt. The mode and the hour were all that occupied or distracted me.

My outstretched hands at length encountered some solid obstruction. It was a wall, seemingly of stone masonry – very smooth, slimy, and cold. I followed it up; stepping with all the careful distrust with which certain antique narratives had inspired me. This process, however, afforded me no means of ascertaining the dimensions of my dungeon, as I might make its circuit and return to the point whence I set out without being aware of the fact, so perfectly uniform seemed the wall. I therefore sought the knife which had been in my pocket when led into the inquisitorial chamber; but it was gone; my clothes had been exchanged for a wrapper of coarse serge. I had thought of forcing the blade in some minute crevice of the masonry, so as to identify my point of departure.

The difficulty, nevertheless, was but trivial; although, in the disorder of my fancy, it seemed at first insuperable. I tore a part of the hem from the robe and placed the fragment at full length, and at right angles to the wall. In groping my way around the prison, I could not fail to encounter this rag upon completing the circuit. So, at least, I thought; but I had not counted upon the extent of the dungeon, or upon my own weakness. The ground was moist and slippery. I staggered onward for some time, when I stumbled and fell. My excessive fatigue induced me to remain prostrate; and sleep soon overtook me as I lay.

Upon awaking, and stretching forth an arm, I found beside me a loaf and a pitcher with water. I was too much exhausted to reflect upon this circumstance, but ate and drank with avidity. Shortly afterward, I resumed my tour around the prison, and with much toil, came at last upon the fragment of the serge. Up to the period when I fell, I had counted fifty-two paces, and, upon resuming my walk, I had counted forty-eight more – when I arrived at the rag. There were in all, then, a hundred paces; and, admitting two paces to the yard, I presumed the dungeon to be fifty yards in circuit. I had met, however, with many angles in the wall, and thus I could form no guess at the shape of the vault, for vault I could not help supposing it to be.

I had little object – certainly no hope – in these researches; but a vague curiosity prompted me to continue them. Quitting the wall, I resolved to cross the area of the enclosure. At first, I proceeded with extreme caution, for the floor, although seemingly of solid material, was treacherous with slime. At length, however, I took courage, and did not hesitate to step firmly – endeavoring to cross in as direct a line as possible. I had advanced some ten or twelve paces in this manner, when the remnant of the torn hem of my robe became entangled between my legs. I stepped on it, and fell violently on my face.

In the confusion attending my fall, I did not immediately apprehend a somewhat startling circumstance, which yet, in a few seconds afterward, and while I still lay prostrate, arrested my attention. It was this; my chin rested upon the floor of the prison, but my lips, and the upper portion of my head, although seemingly at a less elevation than the chin, touched nothing. At the same time, my forehead seemed bathed in a clammy vapor, and the peculiar smell of decayed fungus arose to my nostrils. I put forward my arm, and shuddered to find that I had fallen at the very brink of a circular pit, whose extent, of course, I had no means of ascertaining at the moment. Groping about the masonry just below the margin, I succeeded in dislodging a small fragment, and let it fall into the abyss. For many seconds I hearkened to its reverberations as it dashed against the sides of the chasm in its descent; at length, there was a sullen plunge into water, succeeded by loud echoes. At the same moment, there came a sound resembling the quick opening and as rapid closing of a door overhead, while a faint gleam of light flashed suddenly through the gloom, and as suddenly faded away.

I saw clearly the doom which had been prepared for me, and congratulated myself upon the timely accident by which I had escaped. Another step before my fall, and the world had seen me no more. And the death just avoided was of that very character which I had regarded as fabulous and frivolous in the tales respecting the Inquisition. To the victims of its tyranny, there was the choice of death with its direst physical agonies, or death with its most hideous moral horrors. I had been reserved for the latter. By long suffering my nerves had been unstrung, until I trembled at the sound of my own voice, and had become in every respect a fitting subject for the species of torture which awaited me.

Shaking in every limb, I groped my way back to the wall – resolving there to perish rather than risk the terrors of the wells, of which my imagination now pictured many in various positions about the dungeon. In other conditions of mind, I might have had courage to end my misery at once, by a plunge into one of these abysses; but now I was the veriest of cowards. Neither could I forget what I had read of these pits – that the *sudden* extinction of life formed no part of their most horrible plan.

Agitation of spirit kept me awake for many long hours, but at length I again slumbered. Upon arousing, I found by my side, as before, a loaf and a pitcher of water. A burning thirst consumed me, and I emptied the vessel at a draught. It must have been drugged – for scarcely had I drunk, before I became irresistibly drowsy. A deep sleep fell upon me – a sleep like that of death. How long it lasted, of course I know not; but when, once again, I unclosed my eyes, the objects around me were visible. By a wild, sulphurous lustre, the origin of which I could not at first determine, I was enabled to see the extent and aspect of the prison.

In its size I had been greatly mistaken. The whole circuit of its walls did not exceed twenty-five yards. For some minutes this fact occasioned me a world of vain trouble; vain indeed – for what could be of less importance, under the terrible circumstances which environed me, than the mere dimensions of my dungeon? But my soul took a wild interest in trifles, and I busied myself in endeavors to account for the error I had committed in my measurement. The truth at length flashed upon me. In my first attempt at exploration I had counted fifty-two paces, up to the period when I fell: I must then have been within a pace or two of the fragment of serge; in fact, I had nearly performed the circuit of the vault. I then slept – and, upon waking, I must have returned upon my steps – thus supposing the circuit nearly double what it actually was. My confusion of mind prevented me from observing that I began my tour with the wall to the left, and ended it with the wall to the right.

I had been deceived, too, in respect to the shape of the enclosure. In feeling my way I had found many angles, and thus deduced an idea of great irregularity; so potent is the effect of total darkness upon one arousing from lethargy or sleep! The angles were simply those of a few slight depressions, or niches, at odd intervals. The general shape of the prison was square. What I had taken for masonry seemed now to be iron, or some other metal, in huge plates, whose sutures or joints occasioned the depression. The entire surface of this metallic enclosure was rudely daubed in all the hideous and repulsive devices to which the charnel superstition of the monks has given rise. The figures of fiends in aspects of menace, with skeleton forms, and other more really fearful images, overspread and disfigured the walls. I observed that the outlines of these monstrosities were sufficiently distinct, but that the colors seemed faded and blurred, as if from the effects of a damp atmosphere. I now noticed the floor, too, which was of stone. In the centre yawned the circular pit from whose jaws I had escaped, but it was the only one in the dungeon.

All this I saw indistinctly and by much effort – for my personal condition had been greatly changed during slumber. I now lay upon my back, and at full length, on a species of low framework of wood. To this I was securely bound by a long strap resembling a surcingle. It passed in many convolutions about my limbs and body, leaving at liberty only my head, and my left arm to such extent, that I could, by dint of much exertion, supply myself with food from an earthen dish which lay by my side on the floor. I saw, to my horror, that the pitcher had been removed. I say to my horror – for I was consumed with intolerable thirst. This thirst it appeared to be the design of my persecutors to stimulate – for the food in the dish was meat pungently seasoned.

Looking upward, I surveyed the ceiling of my prison. It was some thirty or forty feet overhead, and constructed much as the side walls. In one of its panels a very singular figure riveted my whole attention. It was the painted figure of Time as he is commonly represented, save that, in lieu of a scythe, he held what, at a casual glance, I supposed to be the pictured image of a huge pendulum, such as we see on antique clocks. There was something, however, in the appearance of this machine which caused me to regard it more attentively. While I gazed directly upward at it (for its position was immediately over my own) I fancied that I saw it in motion. In an instant afterward the fancy was confirmed. Its sweep was brief, and of course slow. I watched it for some minutes somewhat in fear, but more in wonder. Wearied at length with observing its dull movement, I turned my eyes upon the other objects in the cell.

A slight noise attracted my notice, and, looking to the floor, I saw several enormous rats traversing it. They had issued from the well which lay just within view to my right. Even then, while I gazed, they came up in troops, hurriedly, with ravenous eyes, allured by the scent of the meat. From this it required much effort and attention to scare them away.

It might have been half an hour, perhaps even an hour (for I could take but imperfect note of time), before I again cast my eyes upward. What I then saw confounded and amazed me. The sweep of the pendulum had increased in extent by nearly a yard. As a natural consequence its velocity was also much greater. But what mainly disturbed me was the idea that it had perceptibly *descended*. I now observed – with what horror it is needless to say – that its nether extremity was formed of a crescent of glittering steel, about a foot in length from horn to horn; the horns upward, and the under edge evidently as keen as that of a razor. Like a razor also, it seemed massy and heavy, tapering from the edge into a solid and broad structure above. It was appended to a weighty rod of brass, and the whole *hissed* as it swung through the air.

I could no longer doubt the doom prepared for me by monkish ingenuity in torture. My cognizance of the pit had become known to the inquisitorial agents – *the pit*, whose horrors had been destined for so bold a recusant as myself – *the pit*, typical of hell and regarded by rumor as the Ultima Thule of all their punishments. The plunge into this pit I had avoided by the merest of accidents, and I knew that surprise, or entrapment into torment, formed an important portion of all the grotesquerie of these dungeon deaths. Having failed to fall, it was no part of the demon plan to hurl me into the abyss, and thus (there being no alternative) a different and a milder destruction awaited me. Milder! I half smiled in my agony as I thought of such application of such a term.

What boots it to tell of the long, long hours of horror more than mortal, during which I counted the rushing oscillations of the steel! Inch by inch – line by line – with a descent only appreciable at intervals that seemed ages – down and still down it came! Days passed – it might have been that many days passed – ere it swept so closely over me as to fan me with its acrid breath. The odor of the sharp steel forced itself into my nostrils. I prayed – I wearied heaven with my prayer for its more speedy descent. I grew frantically mad, and struggled to force myself upward against the sweep of the fearful scimitar. And then I fell suddenly calm, and lay smiling at the glittering death, as a child at some rare bauble.

There was another interval of utter insensibility; it was brief; for, upon again lapsing into life, there had been no perceptible descent in the pendulum. But it might have been long – for I knew there were demons who took note of my swoon, and who could have arrested the vibration at pleasure. Upon my recovery, too, I felt very – oh! inexpressibly – sick and weak, as if through long inanition. Even amid the agonies of that period, the human nature craved food. With painful effort I outstretched my left arm as far as my bonds permitted, and took possession of the small remnant which had been spared me by the rats. As I put a portion of it within my lips, there rushed to my mind a half-formed thought of joy – of hope. Yet what business had *I* with hope? It was, as I say, a half-formed thought – man has many such, which are never completed. I felt that it was of joy – of hope; but I felt also that it had perished in its formation. In vain I struggled to perfect – to regain it. Long suffering had nearly annihilated all my ordinary powers of mind. I was an imbecile – an idiot.

The vibration of the pendulum was at right angles to my length. I saw that the crescent was designed to cross the region of the heart. It would fray the serge of my robe – it would return and repeat its operations – again – and again. Notwithstanding its terrifically wide sweep (some thirty feet or more), and the hissing vigor of its descent, sufficient to sunder these very walls of iron, still the fraying of my robe would be all that, for several minutes, it would accomplish. And at this thought I paused. I dared not go further than this reflection. I dwelt upon it with a pertinacity of attention – as if, in so dwelling, I could arrest *here* the descent of the steel. I forced myself to ponder upon the sound of the crescent as it should pass across the garment – upon the peculiar thrilling sensation which the friction of cloth produces on the nerves. I pondered upon all this frivolity until my teeth were on edge.

Down – steadily down it crept. I took a frenzied pleasure in contrasting its downward with its lateral velocity. To the right – to the left – far and wide – with the shriek of a damned spirit! to my heart, with the stealthy pace of the tiger! I alternately laughed and howled, as the one or the other idea grew predominant.

Down – certainly, relentlessly down! It vibrated within three inches of my bosom! I struggled violently – furiously – to free my left arm. This was free only from the elbow to the hand. I could reach the latter, from the platter beside me, to my mouth, with great effort, but no farther. Could I have broken the fastenings above the elbow, I would have seized and attempted to arrest the pendulum. I might as well have attempted to arrest an avalanche!

Down – still unceasingly – still inevitably down! I gasped and struggled at each vibration. I shrunk convulsively at its every sweep. My eyes followed its outward or upward whirls with the eagerness of the most unmeaning despair; they closed

themselves spasmodically at the descent, although
death would have been a relief, oh, how unspeakable! Still I quivered in every nerve to think how
slight a sinking of the machinery would precipitate
that keen, glistening axe upon my bosom. It was
hope that prompted the nerve to quiver – the
frame to shrink. It was *hope* – the hope that
triumphs on the rack – that whispers to the death-
condemned even in the dungeons of the
Inquisition.

I saw that some ten or twelve vibrations would
bring the steel in actual contact with my robe –
and with this observation there suddenly came
over my spirit all the keen, collected calmness of
despair. For the first time during many hours – or
perhaps days – I *thought*. It now occurred to me,
that the bandage, or surcingle, which enveloped
me, was *unique*. I was tied by no separate cord.
The first stroke of the razor-like crescent athwart
any portion of the band would so detach it that it
might be unwound from my person by means of
my left hand. But how fearful, in that case, the
proximity of the steel! The result of the slightest
struggle, how deadly! Was it likely, moreover,
that the minions of the torturer had not foreseen
and provided for this possibility? Was it probable
that the bandage crossed my bosom in the track of
the pendulum? Dreading to find my faint and, as
it seemed, my last hope frustrated, I so far elevated
my head as to obtain a distinct view of my breast.
The surcingle enveloped my limbs and body close

in all directions – *save in the path of the destroying crescent*.

Scarcely had I dropped my head back into its original position, when there flashed upon my mind what I cannot better describe than as the unformed half of that idea of deliverance to which I have previously alluded, and of which a moiety only floated indeterminately through my brain when I raised food to my burning lips. The whole thought was now present – feeble, scarcely sane, scarcely definite – but still entire. I proceeded at once, with the nervous energy of despair, to attempt its execution.

For many hours the immediate vicinity of the low framework upon which I lay had been literally swarming with rats. They were wild, bold, ravenous – their red eyes glaring upon me as if they waited but for motionlessness on my part to make me their prey. 'To what food,' I thought, 'have they been accustomed in the well?'

They had devoured, in spite of all my efforts to prevent them, all but a small remnant of the contents of the dish. I had fallen into an habitual see-saw or wave of the hand about the platter; and, at length, the unconscious uniformity of the movement deprived it of effect. In their voracity, the vermin frequently fastened their sharp fangs in my fingers. With the particles of the oily and spicy viand which now remained, I thoroughly rubbed the bandage wherever I could reach it;

then, raising my hand from the floor, I lay breathlessly still.

At first, the ravenous animals were startled and terrified at the change – at the cessation of movement. They shrank alarmedly back; many sought the well. But this was only for a moment. I had not counted in vain upon their voracity. Observing that I remained without motion, one or two of the boldest leaped upon the framework, and smelt at the surcingle. This seemed the signal for a general rush. Forth from the well they hurried in fresh troops. They clung to the wood – they overran it, and leaped in hundreds upon my person. The measured movement of the pendulum disturbed them not at all. Avoiding its strokes, they busied themselves with the anointed bandage. They pressed – they swarmed upon me in ever accumulating heaps. They writhed upon my throat; their cold lips sought my own; I was half stifled by their thronging pressure; disgust, for which the world has no name, swelled my bosom, and chilled, with a heavy clamminess, my heart. Yet one minute, and I felt that the struggle would be over. Plainly I perceived the loosening of the bandage. I knew that in more than one place it must be already severed. With a more than human resolution I lay *still*.

Nor had I erred in my calculations – nor had I endured in vain. I at length felt that I was *free*. The surcingle hung in ribands from my body. But the stroke of the pendulum already pressed upon my bosom. It had divided the serge of the robe. It had cut through the linen beneath. Twice again it swung, and a sharp sense of pain shot through every nerve. But the moment of escape had arrived. At a wave of my hand my deliverers hurried tumultuously away. With a steady movement – cautious, side-long, shrinking, and slow – I slid from the embrace of the bandage and beyond the reach of the scimitar. For the moment, at least, *I was free.*

Free! – and in the grasp of the Inquisition! I had scarcely stepped from my wooden bed of horror upon the stone floor of the prison, when the motion of the hellish machine ceased, and I beheld it drawn up, by some invisible force, through the ceiling. This was a lesson which I took desperately to heart. My every motion was undoubtedly watched. Free! – I had but escaped death in one form of agony, to be delivered unto worse than death in some other. With that thought I rolled my eyes nervously around on the barriers of iron that hemmed me in. Something unusual – some change which, at first, I could not appreciate distinctly – it was obvious, had taken place in the apartment. For many minutes of a dreamy and trembling abstraction, I busied myself in vain, unconnected conjecture. During this period, I became aware, for the first time, of the origin of the sulphurous light which illumined the cell. It proceeded from a fissure, about half an inch in width, extending entirely around the prison at the base of the walls, which thus appeared, and were completely separated from the floor. I endeavored, but of course in vain, to look through the aperture.

As I arose from the attempt, the mystery of the alteration in the chamber broke at once upon my understanding. I have observed that, although the outlines of the figures upon the walls were sufficiently distinct, yet the colors seemed blurred and indefinite. These colors had now assumed, and were momentarily assuming, a startling and most intense brilliancy, that gave to the spectral and fiendish portraitures an aspect that might have thrilled even firmer nerves than my own. Demon eyes, of a wild and ghastly vivacity, glared upon me in a thousand directions, where none had been visible before, and gleamed with the lurid lustre of a fire that I could not force my imagination to regard as usual.

Unreal! – Even while I breathed there came to my nostrils the breath of the vapor of heated iron! A suffocating odor pervaded the prison! A deeper glow settled each moment in the eyes that glared at my agonies! A richer tint of crimson diffused itself over the pictured horrors of blood. I panted! I gasped for breath! There could be no doubt of the design of my tormentors – oh! most unrelenting! oh! most demoniac of men! I shrank from the glowing metal to the centre of the cell. Amid the thought of the fiery destruction that impended, the idea of the coolness of the well came over my soul like balm. I rushed to its deadly brink. I threw my straining vision below. The glare from the enkindled roof illumined its inmost recesses. Yet, for a wild moment, did my spirit refuse to comprehend the meaning of what I saw. At length it forced – it wrestled its way into my soul – it burned itself in upon my shuddering reason. Oh! for a voice to speak! – oh! horror! – oh! any horror but this! With a shriek, I rushed from the margin, and buried my face in my hands – weeping bitterly.

The heat rapidly increased, and once again I looked up, shuddering as with a fit of the ague. There had been a second change in the cell – and now the change was obviously in the *form*. As before, it was in vain that I at first endeavored to appreciate or understand what was taking place. But not long was I left in doubt. The Inquisitorial vengeance had been hurried by my two-fold escape, and there was to be no more dallying with the King of Terrors. The room had been square. I saw that two of its iron angles were now acute – two, consequently, obtuse. The fearful difference quickly increased with a low rumbling or moaning sound. In an instant the apartment had shifted its form into that of a lozenge. But the alteration stopped not here – I neither hoped nor desired it to stop. I could have clasped the red walls to my bosom as a garment of eternal peace. 'Death,' I said, 'any death but that of the pit!' Fool! might I not have known that *into the pit* it was the object of the burning iron to urge me? Could I resist its glow? or if even that, could I withstand its pressure? And now, flatter and flatter grew the lozenge, with a rapidity that left me no time for contemplation. Its centre, and of course its greatest width, came just over the yawning gulf. I shrank back – but the closing walls pressed me resistlessly onward. At length for my seared and writhing body there was no longer an inch of foothold on the firm floor of the prison. I struggled no more, but the agony of my soul found vent in one loud, long, and final scream of despair. I felt that I tottered upon the brink – I averted my eyes –

There was a discordant hum of human voices! There was a loud blast as of many trumpets! There was a harsh grating as of a thousand thunders! The fiery walls rushed back! An outstretched arm caught my own as I fell, fainting, into the abyss. It was that of General Lasalle. The French army had entered Toledo. The Inquisition was in the hands of its enemies.

FRANKENSTEIN
Mary Shelley

Victor Frankenstein, a Swiss scientist, has a great
ambition: to create intelligent life. But when his
creature first stirs, he realizes he has made a
monster. A monster which, abandoned by its
maker and shunned by everyone who sees it, dogs
Dr Frankenstein with murder and horrors to the
very ends of the earth . . .

THE PHANTOM OF THE OPERA
Gaston Leroux

The legendary rumours of an 'opera ghost' take on
a terrifying reality when the beautiful young singer,
Christine Daaé, suddenly disappears after her
triumphant performance. An ever increasing
pattern of fear and violence pervades the dim
backstage areas and subterranean passages of the
glorious Opera House as the phantom threatens to
strike once more.

THE STRANGE CASE OF DR JEKYLL AND MR HYDE *AND* THE SUICIDE CLUB
Robert Louis Stevenson

Dr Jekyll is a respectable, well-liked scientist – until a secret experiment goes hideously wrong, and he is plunged into a nightmare existence as the monstrous Mr Hyde . . . And the hero of The Suicide Club gets just as entangled with a sinister secret society when he unwisely indulges his taste for adventure.

THE HOUND OF THE BASKERVILLES
Sir Arthur Conan Doyle

When Sir Charles Baskerville is found mysteriously dead in the grounds of Baskerville Hall, everyone remembers the legend of the monstrous creature that haunts the moor. The greatest detective in the world, Sherlock Holmes knows there must be a more rational explanation – but the difficulty is to find it before the hellhound finds him . . .

THE GREAT ADVENTURES
OF SHERLOCK HOLMES
Sir Arthur Conan Doyle

From the strange case of The Red-Headed League to the extraordinary tale of The Engineer's Thumb, Sherlock Holmes and his assistant Dr Watson grapple with treachery, murder, and ingenious crimes of all kinds. But no case is too challenging, no mystery unsolvable, for the immortal detective's unique powers of deduction.

THE MYSTERIOUS ADVENTURES
OF SHERLOCK HOLMES
Sir Arthur Conan Doyle

Sherlock Holmes, the great genius of detection, with his assistant Dr Watson, once more attempts to solve the unsolvable. From the extraordinary case of The Resident Patient to the sinister tale of The Crooked Man, Holmes unravels the most challenging of mysteries. Using his astounding methods of deduction, he outwits the most cunning of thieves and most villainous of murderers.

TWENTY THOUSAND LEAGUES UNDER THE SEA
Jules Verne

A mission to rid the seas of a monster becomes a
nightmare for Professor Aronnax, Conseil and
harpooner Ned Land when they become prisoners
of the 'monster' itself – a spectacular submarine
ship commanded by Captain Nemo. But the
marvels of their underwater journey soon distract
them from their worries – the Professor, at least,
wouldn't have missed this voyage for the world!

JOURNEY TO THE CENTRE OF THE EARTH
Jules Verne

When Axel deciphers an old parchment that
describes a secret passage through a volcano to the
centre of the earth, nothing will stop his eccentric
Uncle Lidenbrock from setting out at once. So,
with silent Hans the guide, the two men embark
on a perilous, astonishing, terrifying journey
through the subterranean world – the most
incredible voyage ever!

MOONFLEET
J. Meade Falkner

Everyone in the tiny village of Moonfleet lives by
the sea one way or another, so it's no surprise
when young John Trenchard gets involved in the
smuggling trade. Forced to flee England with a
price on his head, John little guesses the
adventures and trials he will face before he sees
Moonfleet again – or the change in his fortunes
when he does.

THE CORAL ISLAND
R. M. Ballantyne

Fifteen-year-old Ralph, mischievous young
Peterkin and clever, brave Jack are shipwrecked on
a coral reef with only a telescope and a broken
penknife between them. At first the island seems a
paradise, with its plentiful foods and wealth of
natural wonders. But then a party of cannibals
arrives, and after that a pirate ship . . .

GULLIVER'S TRAVELS
Jonathan Swift

Gulliver sees life from many different perspectives during the course of his exciting voyages around the world. In Lilliput he is a giant among a race of little people only six inches high; in Brobdingnag, he himself seems tiny compared to the giant inhabitants, and in the country of the Houyhnhnms, horses rule and humans have the status of animals. Life back in England seems very ordinary after all that he has seen.

SINBAD THE SAILOR AND OTHER TALES FROM THE ARABIAN NIGHTS
Retold by N. J. Dawood

Sindbad, shipwrecked on exotic shores inhabited by mythical beasts and flying men; the amazing adventures of the Barber of Baghdad's six brothers; how Ali Baba outwitted the forty thieves . . . The daily entertainment of everyday people over a thousand years ago, these Arabian, Indian and Persian tales are full of magic and excitement.

KING SOLOMON'S MINES
H. Rider Haggard

Three men trek to the remote African interior in search of a lost friend – and reach, at the end of a perilous journey, an unknown land cut off from the world, where terrible dangers threaten anyone who ventures near the spectacular diamond mines of King Solomon . . .

THE LAST OF THE MOHICANS
James Fenimore Cooper

A classic fast-paced adventure set in the beautiful but harsh surroundings of the American frontier.

Hawk-eye, a white man raised among Indians, and his Mohican Indian friend Chingachgook share a life of peace and seclusion in the wilderness. But the brutal French and Indian war of 1757 forces them from their exile when they agree to guide two sisters to their father's fort, through hostile Indian country.

THE RED BADGE OF COURAGE
Stephen Crane

Young Henry Fleming had always dreamt of
performing heroic deeds in battle. But the reality,
as a raw recruit in the American Civil War, is a
mental and physical torment. And as Henry fights
his inner battles with fear, self-doubt, trauma and
vainglory throughout his first harrowing action, he
has no idea whether war will make him a coward, a
hero – or a man.

THE COUNT OF MONTE CRISTO
Alexandre Dumas

Young Edmond Dantes has everything to look
forward to – he is soon to be captain of his own
ship and to marry his beloved Mercedes. But his
future is cruelly blighted when spiteful enemies
provoke his wrongful arrest and he is condemned
to lifelong imprisonment. Dantes' fate seems
sealed. How can he avenge his accusers and
reverse his fortune? The answer lies hidden on the
Island of Monte Cristo . . .

This epic story has been specially abridged for
Puffin Classics.

AROUND THE WORLD IN EIGHTY DAYS
Jules Verne

For a bet, Phileas Fogg sets out with his servant
Passepartout to achieve an incredible journey –
from London to Paris, Brindisi, Suez, Bombay,
Calcutta, Singapore, Hong Kong, San Francisco,
New York and back to London again, all in just
eighty days! There are many alarms and surprises
along the way – and a last-minute setback that
makes all the difference between winning and
losing.

TOM BROWN'S SCHOOLDAYS
Thomas Hughes

The story of Tom's career at Rugby, from his first
nervous day as a newcomer to his last cricket
match as Captain of the School eleven, introduced
the first believable schoolboy in literature. Tom's
adventures and dilemmas – the childish scrapes,
the bullying, the incomprehensible school
traditions, and the sporting triumphs and disasters
– will still strike a chord with schoolchildren.

THE ADVENTURES OF HUCKLEBERRY FINN
Mark Twain

When Huckleberry Finn runs away from his brutal
father, he meets up with an old friend, the slave
Jim, who is also running away. Together, they
travel by raft down the Mississippi, tumbling in
and out of amazing experiences – from a floating
house to a funeral, a shipwreck to a circus – and
learn some of the strange ways of people in the
Deep South.

THE ADVENTURES OF TOM SAWYER
Mark Twain

Tom skips school and has some incredible
adventures with his friends Huckleberry Finn and
Joe Harper – some real enough, others not quite.
They go off and live like pirates on an island, are
presumed dead, and return just in time for their
own funeral. They witness a murder, and discover
treasure beyond their wildest dreams.

THE THREE MUSKETEERS
Alexandre Dumas

When hot-blooded young d'Artagnan comes to
Paris to seek his fortune, he finds himself
challenged to a duel with not one, but three of the
King's Musketeers. But Athos, Porthos and
Aramis are to become his greatest friends, and
companions in dangerous adventure when he
becomes embroiled in the intrigues of the Court
and the beautiful, evil Lady de Winter.

THE HUNCHBACK OF NOTRE-DAME
Victor Hugo

Outcast by society because of his hideous
appearance, Quasimodo lives under the protection
of his foster father, Claude Frollo, and the
cathedral of Notre-Dame itself. His world revolves
around his fifteen bells and Frollo. But once the
beautiful gypsy girl, La Esmerelda, enters their
lives, all begins to crumble and things can never
return to the way they were.

This epic story has been specially abridged for
Puffin Classics.

THE CALL OF THE WILD
Jack London

Buck is a dog born to luxury, but betrayed and sold to be a sledge dog in the harsh and frozen Yukon. This is the remarkable story of how Buck rises above his enemies to become one of the most feared and admired dogs in the north.

WHITE FANG
Jack London

In the desolate, frozen wilds of north-west Canada, a wolf-cub soon finds himself the sole survivor of the litter. Son of Kiche – half-wolf, half-dog – and the ageing wolf One Eye, he is thrust into a savage world where each day becomes a fight to stay alive.

READ MORE IN PUFFIN

For children of all ages, Puffin represents quality and variety – the very best in publishing today around the world.

For complete information about books available from Puffin – and Penguin – and how to order them, contact us at the appropriate address below. Please note that for copyright reasons the selection of books varies from country to country.

On the world wide web: www.penguin.co.uk

In the United Kingdom: Please write to *Dept. EP, Penguin Books Ltd, Bath Road, Harmondsworth, West Drayton, Middlesex UB7 ODA*
Schools Line in the UK: Please write to

In the United States: Please write to *Consumer Sales, Penguin USA, P.O. Box 999, Dept. 17109, Bergenfield, New Jersey 07621-0120.* VISA and MasterCard holders call 1-800-253-6476 to order Penguin titles

In Canada: Please write to *Penguin Books Canada Ltd, 10 Alcorn Avenue, Suite 300, Toronto, Ontario M4V 3B2*

In Australia: Please write to *Penguin Books Australia Ltd, P.O. Box 257, Ringwood, Victoria 3134*

In New Zealand: Please write to *Penguin Books (NZ) Ltd, Private Bag 102902, North Shore Mail Centre, Auckland 10*

In India: Please write to *Penguin Books India Pvt Ltd, 706 Eros Apartments, 56 Nehru Place, New Delhi 110 019*

In the Netherlands: Please write to *Penguin Books Netherlands bv, Postbus 3507, NL-1001 AH Amsterdam*

In Germany: Please write to *Penguin Books Deutschland GmbH, Metzlerstrasse 26, 60594 Frankfurt am Main*

In Spain: Please write to *Penguin Books S. A., Bravo Murillo 19, 1° B, 28015 Madrid*

In Italy: Please write to *Penguin Italia s.r.l., Via Felice Casati 20, I–20124 Milano*

In France: Please write to *Penguin France S. A., 17 rue Lejeune, F–31000 Toulouse*

In Japan: Please write to *Penguin Books Japan, Ishikiribashi Building, 2–5–4, Suido, Bunkyo-ku, Tokyo 112*

In South Africa: Please write to *Longman Penguin Southern Africa (Pty) Ltd, Private Bag X08, Bertsham 2013*